ORDINARY BOY

ORDINARY BOY

To Madeline –
An extraordinary young woman!
Stacey Longo

Stacey Longo

Dark Alley Press

ORDINARY BOY

ISBN: 978-0-692-35282-3

Dark Alley Press
http://www.darkalleypress.com

An imprint of Vagabondage Press LLC
PO Box 3563
Apollo Beach, Florida 33572
http://www.vagabondagepress.com

First edition printed in the United States of America and the United Kingdom, March 2015

10 9 8 7 6 5 4 3 2 1

Front cover images by Soupstock, Dudarev Mikhail, and Rasica. Cover designed by Maggie Ward.

ORDINARY BOY

In memory of T.N.

Many thanks to my researcher, Dennis Cole; my colleagues, Nick Cato, Dan Foley, Ryann George, Dale T. Phillips, Kristi Petersen Schoonover, Ken Strobel, John Valeri, Vlad Vaslyn, and Ursula Wong, for your critique and feedback; and my family and husband, for living with this story as long as you have.

ORDINARY BOY

PROLOGUE

A little about me: Until my extraordinary death, I live an ordinary life. I am the boy that nobody sees, ignored in the shadows of the hallway. I am the kid that is picked last in gym. I am the student that is never called on in class to answer the question, and, after a while, I stop bothering to raise my hand.

It is not until my stepfather shoots me that I am finally—*finally*—noticed.

Before I meet my untimely end, let me start at the beginning.

1.

We live in Osprey Falls, Maine, which Mom says is the most pretentious name for a town this side of the Connecticut River. Our mustard-colored duplex is in the part of town called The Meadows, which is where all the poor people live. Nana lives in the other half of our duplex.

The Meadows is as close to the edge of town as you can get. Mom says when the local Democrats finally won their bid to put up low-income housing so the less privileged could enjoy the fineries of Osprey Falls, too, the doctors and lawyers who made up the town decided the development would be built as far from their colonials and pristine white capes as possible. We're on the border of Osprey Falls and East Bailey, which everyone knows is a hole. It's definitely better to be from Osprey Falls than East Bailey, even if we're just spitting distance from the town line.

The first thing you see when you turn in to The Meadows entrance is the Quick-E-Mart on the corner. That's where Nana works. They sell everything from milk to Odor Eaters. They also sell Twinkies for 27 cents a pack. This drives Bobby Foley crazy, because he only gets 25 cents a week allowance from his father. He's always walking with his eyes glued to the ground, looking for stray pennies so he doesn't have to wait an extra week to buy his Twinkies.

We don't get an allowance, because Mom says we should do our chores just because we're good people and not for money. It's not that big of a deal, though, because Nana saves all the Twinkies that are out of date and brings them home for us, so we don't need to pay for them. Once in a while, she'll get a fruit pie or a Ring Ding, too, but never Sno-balls. Those always sell out before they get a chance to expire, which figures, since they're my favorite.

My parents, Stephen and Stephanie Barracato, divorced four years ago when I was four and Sally was six. I never thought it was fair that everyone in my family got to have an "S" name except me, Curtis. Mom says I was named after my grandfather, Francis Curtis Barracato, but he died when I was a baby, and I don't see why she couldn't have changed my name after his funeral.

Sally has straight, blond hair and blue eyes like Mom, and I have stringy, brown hair and blue eyes like Dad. Sometimes Sally tries to tell me I am adopted, and I really don't belong to our family, but whenever Mom hears her, she just rolls her eyes and says I'm the mirror image of my father; no way I'm not theirs.

When Dad left and Mom had to move to The Meadows because that's all she could afford on her salary as a K-Mart clerk, she made us change our last name back to hers: Price. I was sore about that when I got a little older and was able to think about it some. Barracato almost sounds like barracuda, which is a much cooler name than Price, which rhymes with lice, which Bobby Foley was pretty quick to figure out. But Mom didn't want any reminders of Dad around, not even his name, so I remained ordinary Curtis Price, from the poor side of town.

Mom is still pretty mad at Dad for leaving us. Nana tells her all the time that she shouldn't complain about him in front of Sally and me, but Mom says she can't help herself. When Mom and Dad were first married, they lived in a nice house outside of Bangor, but then Dad lost his job as a deliveryman for Coca-Cola and had to go to work selling vacuum cleaners door-to-door. Mom says Dad was fooling around with one of the people he sold a vacuum to, and that's why he left. I guess when you're a grown-up, you can't fool around and play games like you can when you're a kid. Mom plays Go Fish and War with me and Sally, but she says it's not the same thing. Nana's always telling Mom she should try to meet a nice man, but Mom says the next guy she marries is going to have to be a lot different from every other man she's ever met. She says she wants someone who surprises her. I tried to surprise her once by putting a toad in the sink, and she sent me to bed without dinner, so I don't know what she's talking about. Mom doesn't seem to like surprises at all.

Now that I'm eight, I'm allowed to hang out outside without Nana or Mom watching me from the front step. We have our own group of friends in the neighborhood. There's Danny and David Ewing, identical twins the same age as Sally: ten. I never get their names straight, but I think Danny's the one who parts his bristly brown hair on the left. I just can't remember if it's his left or my left. They have a little sister, Peggy, who doesn't talk much, and always has her nose stuck in a book.

Jill Jackson is the only other girl in the neighborhood Sally's age. She has chocolate skin and wears her hair in two thick ponytails. Her mother puts extra elastic bands all through her pigtails, so it looks like she has two chains of silky black cotton balls sticking out of her head. Jill is nice enough, but sometimes she and Sally ignore me or call me a doofus for no good reason, just because I want to hang out with them.

Bobby Foley is a mean jerk, but he's also the only boy in the neighborhood who's my age, so I put up with him. Bobby's dad cuts his jet-black hair in a square buzz cut, like he's already destined to be a soldier someday. Bobby likes to go in to the Quick-E, open up the saltine crackers, and steal a sleeve of them right out of the box. He's got a floppy-eared beagle named Lady, and he likes to pull on her ears and try and ride her like a horse. He's three inches taller than me and two times as wide, and you can tell by looking at her that Lady just wants to die every time Bobby tries to sit on her squatty little back. She lets out a yelp and runs away as fast as she can, but Bobby is usually right behind her, throwing rocks and calling her a bad dog.

Bobby lives with his dad two houses down from us and Nana. His dad works all night and sleeps all day, so we can never play in his yard. Whenever we are too loud and too close to the house, Bobby's dad comes out and clips Bobby right in the face. One time Bobby's dad hit him so hard one of his eyes went blood red for a week. We usually hang out at my house or at the baseball field at the far end of the development.

And there's Allison Bingham, but everyone calls her Stinky Pinky on account of the pink birthmark that starts on her chin and reaches down her neck. She has dirty blond hair, but on her face, the fine hair appears white against the red and looks so soft that sometimes I catch myself staring, wondering what it would feel like to pet her birthmark. She'd be the outcast of the group except she makes us an even eight, which comes in handy for scrimmage kickball games or Capture-the-Flag.

When I'm not with the neighborhood gang, I'm with Nana. She's my mother's mother. Nana is big and soft and warm and always hugs me when I visit her side of the duplex. She always has lots of warm ginger ale and stale tortilla chips, which she puts on the table when Sally and I come over. Nana's got short hair that she wears real curly. She says she uses a blond rinse in it to keep her looking young, but her hair looks white to me. Occasionally, though, if she's settling in to a lawn chair in the back yard, her hair looks yellow when the sun hits her curls.

Nana tells me stories about my Pop-Pop Henry, who died before I was born. Pop-Pop was sixteen and Nana was fourteen the first time they met, when Nana went over to his farm with her mother to pick strawberries. He told her that first day he was going to marry her. She was terrified that her parents would hear him. Her mother had always told her never to speak to boys, especially ones she didn't know, and here Pop-Pop Henry was, the way Nana tells it, practically proposing to her amid the rows of strawberry plants. But her mother just smiled and told Pop-Pop that perhaps he could come over for dinner after church the next Sunday. It turned out that Pop-Pop's family had a lot of farmland, which Nana's mother thought meant he had a good future ahead of him. They were married when Nana was sixteen years old.

After they were married, Nana found out that Pop-Pop's family owed a lot of money on the land they owned, and when they couldn't pay, the bank took the farm away from them. Pop-Pop went to work as a laborer for a neighboring dairy, and he was a hard worker, but Nana says he was a hard drinker, too. She says if you drink too much, it can kill you, which is what happened to Pop-Pop. I think that means he drowned from the inside out. I hate it when Nana tells that story, because I drink a lot, too. Some days, when I've been hitting balls with the neighborhood gang or playing Red Rover, I might slurp down two full glasses of ice water before remembering how Pop-Pop died from drinking too much. I asked Nana once how you knew if you've had too much, and she said, "If you can't stand up, you've had too much." Then she laughed and told me not to worry; she was sure I was fine.

Nana's the one who I go to whenever I have a question about life. Take Sally: She and I get along fine when we're playing Monopoly or catching fireflies in the back yard, but if anyone else is around, she pretends I'm just about the last person in the world she wants to hang out with and doesn't talk to me at all. Nana says that's because she's my sister and her friends would probably make fun of her for wanting to hang out with her brother instead of them. Nana says this will change when we're older and Sally wants to date my friends. I think that's stupid and gross. Then Nana says when I get older, I might want to date Sally's friends, too, and if Nana ever catches me checking out the girls' "sweet treats," she'll tan my hide and sell me to the Indians. I love my Nana, but if some girl is offering me candy, I'll just make them promise not to tell Nana and then go ahead and have a taste.

Mom has to work through dinnertime most nights, so Nana feeds us and makes sure we take our baths. Then she takes us back next door, tucking us in to our bunk beds in the room Sally and I share, and she runs her hands through our hair to check for ticks. She makes a game out of it, pretending she's a fancy hairdresser massaging our scalps, talking in a high-pitched, frou-frou accent and making us laugh. Nana's nightly tick checks are my favorite part of the day.

2.

School isn't so bad since all of us Meadows kids go to Eastland Elementary together. The good thing about coming from the poor side of town is that everyone seems to be a little bit afraid of us. We travel as a pack, eating lunch at the same table in the cafeteria and taking over the soccer field at recess. Even Stinky Pinky is allowed in our circle, though we don't talk to her as much in school as we do at home. You can overcome being poor in school, but it's hard to overcome looking like a freak, and none of us want her weirdness rubbing off on us. She has to sit one chair away from us at the lunchroom table, but we tell her it's because none of us can stand the smell of the peanut butter and pickle sandwiches she brings every day for lunch. You'd think she'd switch to something else, like straight peanut butter, but she doesn't. I guess she doesn't want to find out the truth—that if she did bring bologna and cheese one day, we'd still make her move one chair down.

We all ride the bus together, and Bobby Foley taught us the words to "We Don't Need No Education," so we all sing this on the ride home after school. We've gone through two different drivers so far. Bobby says he wants to make it an even six before the end of the school year. The way we sing, he might get his way. The driver we have now spends more time peering in the mirror and barking at us to sit down and not switch seats than she does watching the road. Bobby says he's made it his personal mission to break her spirit. He likes to shoot spitballs at the back of her head while she drives, but his aim isn't very good. He's more likely to hit the Ewing twins, who always sit one behind the other in back of the driver. When that happens, Danny and David wait for Bobby to get off the bus after them, and then they pick up clumps of dirt and rocks and throw them at him. Bobby says it's no big deal, but he's usually gritting his teeth pretty hard when he says it, spitting out dirt.

The one day that Nana isn't waiting at the door to greet us after school, Sally is off with Jill, pretending to be spies on a treasure hunt. We're supposed to check in with Nana before we go off with our friends, but Sally always tells me just to tell Nana she's with Jill. That Thursday, Nana doesn't answer the door when I knock on it and call her name. Sally has the spare key, because she's older and more responsible, so I walk around to the back of the house and climb up the propane tank. I can jimmy up the window over Nana's kitchen sink and crawl in from there.

Nana's Scrabble game is laid out on the kitchen table. She likes Scrabble so much that she plays against herself all the time. The board is on a turntable so she just has to spin it to switch sides. The kitchen is empty, but I can hear *General Hospital* on the television in the living room. Nana loves her stories, as she calls them, and she even took the day off of work last year to watch a big wedding on *General Hospital*. She tells me about the people on her show like they're real, and sometimes when she's short-tempered she'll say something like "I'm just mad at that evil Mikkos Cassadine" to explain away her being grouchy.

Nana is in her gray recliner, feet propped up. She's wearing a grayish-white housedress with blue flowers that match her dirty blue slippers. Her mouth is open, like it is when she's snoring, but her eyes are open too.

"Nana?" I ask, but she doesn't answer me. I wonder if there's something wrong with her eyelids, because she hasn't blinked at all since I came in. "Nana? Are you awake?"

She doesn't respond, even when I shake her. Her skin is cool to the touch, like Sally's was this past spring after she had a fever and it broke. I wonder if Nana has a fever, too. She looks awfully pale and maybe a little blue, but she's not sweating like Sally was. And she's totally ignoring me, which isn't funny.

Mom always says that if someone is real sick, you should call the doctor. I don't know any doctors, but I do know their phone number: 9-1-1. I punch in the numbers and tell the woman that answers that my Nana is sick with a fever and won't talk to me.

The doctors that come in the ambulance are really nice to me. The man with the patch that reads EMS takes me out to the back yard and asks me where my mother is. I tell him she's at work, and we're never to call her unless it's an emergency.

"Well, Curtis," the man says, 'cause he asked me my name just a moment ago, "I think this is the kind of thing that your mom would consider an emergency." I fish Mom's work number out of my backpack and hand it to him. Sally is still nowhere to be found, and Nana still hasn't come out to tell me she's not feeling well and going to lie down. I'm starting to get a little bit scared.

Mom finds me in the back yard with EMS. She's got Sally in tow, and I wonder where she found her. I'm exactly where I'm supposed to be, at Nana's after school, but Sally was off with Jill, which she's not supposed to do until she checks in with Nana. I hope Sally is in trouble.

Mom is crying as she hugs me and tells me we have to go inside our house now. Nana's back window is still open where I jimmied it to get in. I tell Mom I left it open, and we have to close it, because Nana doesn't like it when bugs get in the house. Mom shakes her head and cries harder, but she does ask EMS to close it for us. Then we walk three steps to our back door. Mom heats up Spaghetti-Os for dinner and sends us up to bed real early. Sally and I play Fifty Questions and Who Am I? until we're ready to go to sleep.

We have to go to school the next day, but Mom stays home from work. Sally and I come right to the house off the bus, because having Mom there after school is fun for us, usually. But Mom doesn't want to play board games or hide-and-seek with us. She sits us down, real serious at the kitchen table, and tells us Nana has "gone to Heaven to be with Pop-Pop Henry." She won't be next door any more, and we have until the end of the month to pack up Nana's Scrabble board and housecoats and move them to the community center building at the end of the street that all the neighbors use for storage. Starting next week, we have to go over to Danny and David's house after school, and Mom will pay their mother to watch us until she gets home. Mom is going to try to change her schedule at K-Mart so she can be home by dinnertime. Her eyes are red, and she keeps wiping her nose with a Kleenex while she tells us this, and Sally starts to cry, too. I'm not sure what I'm supposed to do, so I get up and hug Mom, which makes her cry even harder. What I want to do is go over to Nana's and see if she's really gone, and if she left any Twinkies for us before she left to go see Pop-Pop.

3.

It's not fair that Nana is gone, and we have to stay with the Ewings after school. Danny and David's mother towers over us, and she has a moustache. She bakes a lot, but we're only allowed one treat after school, a mini-cupcake or a brownie or one cookie. They're always really good, which is awful when our snacks are finished, and we have to stare at the rest of the plate of chocolate frosted cupcakes. Nobody dares to take a second one because Mrs. Ewing will smack your hand with the fly swatter she keeps on top of the refrigerator, always within her reach.

A new neighbor moved in to the other half of our duplex three months after Nana died. His name is Mr. Jervis, and he has a lot of tattoos and wears a lot of gold chains. When he smiles, you can see where he's missing some of his teeth. We can smell the smoke through the walls from the cigar he's always holding. He came over and introduced himself two days after he moved in. He winked at Mom a lot and told her if she ever needed help with anything in the house that she needed a man to do, he'd be happy to lend a hand. Mom smiled without showing her teeth and said that was awful nice of him to offer, but I was the man of the house and could handle anything that came up.

"You kids better keep the noise down," he muttered to me and Sally and left without even taking the glass of water Mom had offered him. He spends most of his time out front, puffing on a stinky cigar and lazily aiming at squirrels with his pellet gun. Sometimes we hear the loud *pop* when he shoots at one, but he must not be very good at it, because I haven't found any splattered in the yard. When he's not hunting down squirrels, he likes to cruise through the neighborhood in his big blue Scout, which kind of looks like an army tank, gunning it when he passes us on the sidewalk like he's going to hit us.

I don't like Mr. Jervis much.

We settle in to our new routine, though, and after days, then months, then a year passes, I start to forget the days when I would come home to Nana and her expired Hostess treats. I don't do it on purpose. But sometimes, Mrs. Ewing will swat at me when I reach out for a second cookie fresh out of the oven, and I think *Nana would've let me have another one … probably.* I'm not quite sure anymore. My afternoons are spent avoiding Mr. Jervis, checking in with Mrs. Ewing, and trying to beat Bobby Foley when we race down to the baseball field and back. It's hard to believe now that there was a time when Nana was always around, waiting for me, every day.

Danny and David and Sally are now all almost twelve, and I just turned ten, so they like to dare me to do stupid stuff to prove I'm not a baby. One day, I have to sneak into Bobby's back yard and knock on the window to try and wake his dad up. I rap on the window as softly as I can, and when Bobby's face appears suddenly, I motion for him to come outside like that's what I'd wanted all along.

Bobby comes out quietly, and we walk back towards the Ewing's house. He kicks a few stones and some dirt up as we go but stops suddenly in front of the house across the street from Danny and David's. It's where Jill lives.

"What's your problem?" I ask, trying to study him out of the corner of my eye, looking for fresh bruises. I don't see any.

He's looking at a dark lump under the tree in front of Jill's. He scowls for a moment, then bends down to pick up a rock and throws it at the gloomy heap. The rock hits it with a soft thud, and the lump remains still. He picks up another rock, lobs it. Another direct hit, and again, no response. I'm curious now, so I step up on Jill's lawn and take a closer look. As I draw near, I gulp. The lump is Lady, lying on her side, just as dead as a turd. "Bobby," I say, meaning to warn him before he gets closer, but he's right behind me, and he shoves me to the side. He squats down. Lady's eyes are open like Nana's were, her tongue is poking out slightly, and there's blood on her hindquarters. I don't know much about dead, but I'm sure Bobby isn't going to be riding that dog again in this lifetime. He stands in one quick motion, turning on me.

"You," he snarls, and I just about wet my pants.

"Um … what?" I say.

"This is your fault," he growls, and I take a step back. Bobby's eyes are narrowed in to slits, and he's making a fist with his right hand. I can't believe it—I think Bobby Foley might actually be ready to cry. I'd think about that a little longer, except I'm pretty sure he's about to beat the snot out of me.

"You killed your Nana and now you killed my dog. You're a bad weed, Curtis Price, and you're gonna pay."

"What? Bobby, I didn't do nothing to Lady, I swear! What are you—" Bobby cuts me off with a fist to my mouth. I feel my teeth crunch. I fall to my knees, right next to Lady, who now has a fly on her eyeball, cleaning its front legs. My face feels like it exploded. There's something hard and pebbly on my tongue, and I spit out a tooth.

"You killed your Nana, and now you got my dog! Bastard!" Bobby cuffs the side of my face this time, and my ear goes hot with pain. I clench my hands, ready to jump on him if he says that about my Nana one more time. I'm so surprised I can't hide my tears fast enough.

"Did not," I sniffle, because it's not true. I loved my Nana so much that I was the one who found her. Sally was off with Jill and should have known something was wrong, which just proves I loved Nana more than her. Bobby hits me again, and now the throbbing in my ear is a sharp stab. I turn my face to him, and he's bright red, tears streaming down his face. He draws his arm back again, ready to pummel me some more.

Now I'm so angry I can't think, so I reach out to grab the only weapon I can find. Lady's body peels stiffly off the ground, and I've got her by the forelegs. I swing her around and catch Bobby square in the jaw with the corpse of his dog.

"She probably jumped in front of a car to get away from you," I scream. Bobby looks stunned, blinking his eyes, and I dart up and across the street. Mrs. Ewing's mouth forms an "O" of surprise as I burst through the door and slam it shut behind me. I lock it quickly and look out the window. Bobby is still standing on Jill's lawn. He reaches down and scoops up Lady's body where I dropped it like he's cradling a baby. He spins on his heel and stalks back to his house.

Bobby Foley is a no-life, and I hate him.

I wind up with a fat lip and a bruise on my face near where Bobby boxed my ear. My ears ring for a few days, but eventually it goes away. Mom tells me she doesn't want me playing with Bobby Foley any more. I tell her that's no problem. Now that his dog is dead, there's nothing really interesting about Bobby Foley anyway.

Sally and I don't want to share a room anymore, but there's no other bedroom for one of us to move to. Sally says she needs her privacy, and quite frankly, she's not a lot of fun to be around these days. She's always giggling and acting stupid when we're with Danny and David, and she doesn't want to play baseball or do anything that might mess up her hair or get her clothes dirty. Mom says she's had it with us and tells me if I can't stop teasing and tormenting my sister, I'm moving into the closet.

The closet! Why didn't I think of it before? Sally and I work it out so I can put my clothes in the closet and my stuff on the shelf above, and she can have the dresser. I pull my twin mattress off the bunk bed and squeeze it in. It just fits. There's a light in there and I have enough room for my comic books and my stuffed dog, Clem. Nobody knows about Clem except Mom and Sally, and Sally won't say anything because she still sleeps with her stuffed monkey, Mr. Jones. We're both pretty happy with our new arrangement.

Mom rolls her eyes at me when she comes in to tuck us in but kneels down obligingly to kiss my forehead. I pull the door up the runners and I'm closed in. Finally I'm alone. I lie on my mattress and hug one of Nana's sweaters that I saved when we were packing her clothes. It still smells a little bit like the Jean Naté powder Nana always wore. Bobby Foley isn't my friend anymore, and Sally is talking about things like boys and shaving her legs, but it's all okay. It's just me and Nana's perfume, safe in my closet.

4.

We see Dad about once a month. Mom says he's supposed to pick us up every other weekend, but Dad has a busy job as a Kirby vacuum cleaner salesman, and he can't always make his weekends with us. I love the Kirby that Dad keeps at his house. It's silver and blue and looks like something that the Jetsons would use.

Dad's apartment is in East Bailey, but Sally and I would rather die than tell anybody that. We usually spend our weekends playing Pac-Man and Centipede on the Atari that Dad picked up from one of his clients. Dad took $100 off of a Kirby for the game system. I think if he'd taken off three times that amount, it still would have been worth it.

Mom often says there's just something about a man with brown hair and blue eyes, and Dad always seems to have a new girlfriend each time we go over, so maybe she's right. I really like his new friend Carrie, who is going to community college to be a nurse. Carrie wears her hair in long, blond waves, and she reminds me of the princess in *Sleeping Beauty*. Dad is starting to go gray, and Carrie is the same age as Becky Billows, the girl who babysits us once in a while when Mom wants to go down to the Emerald for a drink.

Carrie is sitting on the couch one day, sipping a beer and watching Sally destroy my high score at Pac-Man, when I try to strike up a conversation.

"How old are you?" I ask, because I'm curious, and I don't know yet that it's rude to ask a woman her age.

"Twenty," she says with a nervous laugh. She doesn't like talking to Sally and me much.

"And how old is my Dad?" I ask, because I can't remember.

"Thirty-seven," she says. I think about this for a minute. Carrie is twice as old as me, but she is still closer to ten than she is to thirty-seven. That seems a little gross to me. I wouldn't want to marry anyone that old. I don't ever even want to *be* that old. It occurs to me that my father is an old man.

"Why are you hanging out with him?" I ask, because I genuinely want to know. Maybe she doesn't have a dad of her own. But even if that's the case, I don't necessarily want to share mine with her. She can go find someone else's dad to adopt. Bobby Foley's father flashes quickly across my mind. I can introduce Carrie to him if she likes.

Carrie is studying me closely. Her dark eyes crinkle up, and she breaks out in to a wide, crooked grin. She laughs, a throaty purr that starts deep in her chest and spreads out to fill the room. She gets up, wipes her hands on her jean shorts, and musses my brown wavy hair.

"That is a *very* good question. See ya, Curtis." She grabs her backpack and walks out the door. Sally has the Atari on pause, and she's staring at me, wide-eyed and open-mouthed.

"What did you *say* to her?" she asks.

I tell Sally exactly what I said and make her promise not to tell Dad when he gets back from picking up hamburgers and hotdogs from the grocery store. I tell Sally it's okay that Carrie left, because Sally's old enough to watch both of us, which makes her puff up proudly. I'm not stupid. I've heard Sally make the same argument to Mom a hundred times. Sally doesn't want to go over to the Ewing's house anymore, because I heard her tell Jill she let David feel her up and now she's embarrassed to go over there. I don't know what "feel her up" means, exactly, but it makes me think of the balls of clay we get in art class that we have to shape in to ashtrays and cups, and I know how hard I have to press my thumb in to that just to get it to form the right shape. If "feel her up" is anything like that, it certainly doesn't sound fun.

We tell Dad when he gets back that Carrie just up and left, and we can hear him swearing and trying to call her from the bedroom. She doesn't answer, but she must have eventually told him something, because after that, whenever we go over to Dad's for the weekend, he keeps his girlfriends away. This works out great, because it used to be that Dad and his girlfriend would take the bedroom, and Sally and I would fight over who got the couch in the living room and who got the sleeping bag on the floor. I usually wound up on the floor. After scaring Carrie away, I get to share Dad's bed with him, and Sally has the living room all to herself. Sometimes Dad makes up stories to tell me as I fall asleep. There are alien robots and alien cowboys and alien zombies, which would have scared Sally but are right up my alley. I wish we could stay over Dad's every weekend, but when I tell him that, he just rolls his eyes.

As the months go by, Dad has to work more and more, and we don't get to see him hardly at all anymore. Mom starts complaining that he must be so busy he can't even find time to write the child support check. I hear her on the phone with Mrs. Ewing one day when I go into the kitchen for some grape Kool-Aid. Sally likes cherry Kool-Aid, because when she drinks it, her lips turn red and she can pretend she's wearing makeup without Mom yelling at her, but I think grape tastes better. Mom starts whispering when she sees me, but I catch a snippet:

"I don't know what to do, Marilyn. I've already cancelled the cable. Yeah, I did that, but they said they couldn't approve me because they have to consider his child support as part of my income, whether he pays it or not. If I don't pay the power bill by tomorrow, they'll shut the lights off. I don't—" she breaks off, and I look up, and her shoulders are shaking, just a little. She shoos me out of the room.

Later in the day, Mom tells me she's going next door to visit Mr. Jervis. She says she'll only be gone an hour or so, and Sally can watch me. Sally decides to boss me around and make me fold the laundry, which I don't like one bit. As I sort clothes, I can hear Mom giggling through the walls of the duplex, and a little later, she's saying the name George, kind of panting it like she's all out of breath or something. Maybe she and Mr. Jervis went out running. I wish *I* could go for a run right now. I'm tired of matching up socks. Mom comes home just in time to make dinner, her hair mussed and her eyes sad. She's quiet while we eat.

The next day, I remember Mom's conversation with Mrs. Ewing, and figure that whatever Mom said to her must have worked, because our lights are still on.

5.

Sally is such a priss I can barely stand to be around her at all. Ever since turning thirteen, she thinks she walks on water. She took a babysitting class at school and now she watches me all the time in the afternoons. We usually go over to Jill's house, which Mom says is forbidden, but Sally says if I tell, she'll knock all my teeth down my throat until they march out of my butthole single file. She could do it, too.

Jill's hair is real short now and her legs are long and smooth, and Sally's always telling her she could be a supermodel. I know Sally wants her to say the same thing back to her, but Sally's short and bulky and has buckteeth. Sally saved up her babysitting money to get a perm, and now her hair is fuzzy instead of long and straight. Whenever Mom brings home clothes from K-Mart, Sally rips the shoulders and puts holes in the jeans, which makes Mom turn three shades of purple. Sally wears florescent jelly bracelets and legwarmers and thinks she looks just like Madonna on the MTV. We don't get MTV, but Jill does, and most days, right after school, Sally makes the three of us march over to Jill's house to watch an hour of videos. Then Sally and I have to scram out of there, back to our duplex before Jill's mother gets home. Sally wants to marry the lead singer of Duran Duran, and Jill says she'll marry the bass guitarist, and then the two of them can buy houses next door to each other, on the other side of Osprey Falls, where all the really big mansions are. I think the keyboardist of Duran Duran is kind of pretty, but I'm pretty sure he's a guy, so I don't say anything. Sometimes Jill and Sally tease up my hair and put eyeliner on me so I'll look like a glam rocker. I like being included, so I let them do it, but I'd rather die than tell anybody.

Sometimes Sally and Jill lay out in the back yard in their bikinis to try to get a tan. I want to ask Jill why she bothers, since she is already the milkiest of chocolate brown, but I don't want to let on that I don't understand girls at all. Sally wears a bra now but her boobs are kind of fat and floppy. But Jill's look soft and round in her bikini, and sometimes I peek my head out of Mom's bedroom window to look down at her, basking in the sun.

Jill and Sally and the Ewing twins are in middle school now, so our crowd at the lunch table has shifted. It's still all kids from The Meadows, but we had to let some of the younger ones in to fill out the table. Bobby and I rarely sit next to each other, but we can tolerate each other if there's a person or two in between us. Stinky Pinky has made friends with Wanda Wilkes, two years younger than me and one year younger than Pinky. Wanda fills in the chair that used to separate Pinky from the rest of us, so she's almost part of the crowd now. She finally switched sandwiches and usually brings turkey for lunch these days.

I don't have any close friends, really, nobody I swap comic books with or invite over to spy on Sally and Jill. Nana used to be my best friend. The worst is after school, when the kids around the neighborhood get together for a game. We all need to show up in order to have decent teams for kickball. Bobby Foley and I don't speak, and sometimes he spits at my feet. He won't play on the same side as me. He says I smell like death.

I hate Bobby Foley.

I do okay in school, I guess. I got a B in math and English, and a C in art because of those stupid clay ashtrays that we have to make every year. Miss Soling says I didn't put any effort into my latest ashtray, because I didn't paint it with glaze before it went in the kiln. My mom doesn't smoke and my dad quit years ago, so why do I care about a stupid ashtray? I can't wait to move on to papier-mâché. I'm sure I will do awesome at papier-mâché.

On Saturdays, I run errands with Mom. She listens to the oldies station, and I know all the words to "It's My Party" because they play it so much. If she isn't able to do the grocery shopping on Saturday, we go on Sunday, and she lets me listen to Casey Kasem's Top 40

Countdown. I like "The Goonies Are Good Enough" by Cyndi Lauper and "Glory Days" by Bruce Springsteen. Mom says she likes "Every Time You Go Away" by Paul Young. Bruce Springsteen is the coolest guy in the world, and I want to get a pair of blue jeans like his, but Mom says we can't afford it.

We stop at CVS one Saturday to get aspirin, and Mom gasps when she sees *People* magazine at the counter. She buys it even though she was just complaining about how we couldn't afford the brand name Tylenol.

I ask her about the magazine on the ride home, and she tells me the skinny guy on the cover with the big eyes and hollow cheeks is Rock Hudson, some actor she liked when she was younger. She tells me she even paid a dollar and filled out a form to be an official member of the Rock Hudson Fan Club. She still has her membership certificate somewhere. After we get home and she reads the magazine, she frowns a lot. I ask her why she's so sad, and she says there's a new sickness, and Rock Hudson caught it, and there's no cure. I start to get nervous. I have a rash on my thigh that I hadn't said anything about, but now that there's this new sickness, I drop my shorts right there and show Mom.

"Does it look like this? Could I have it?"

Mom smiles and hugs me and says no, that looks like heat rash. She tells me that the only way to catch it is to be with another boy, and when my eyes go wide, she stops.

"Curtis, do you even know what 'gay' means?"

Sometimes Sally and Jill will say things like "that's so gay," but when I tell Mom this, she says no, I don't quite get what gay means. She says that sometimes boys like other boys as more than just friends, and girls like girls romantically, like how I think Pat Benatar is pretty. She says these boys move in with each other and sleep in the same bed and that's how you catch this new sickness. She says that people call these men bad names like "queer" and "fag," but she doesn't ever want to hear me use words like these. Gay people aren't any different than anyone else and can't pick who they fall in love with, just like us. In fact, she adds, her cousin Julia, who we haven't seen since Nana's funeral, is gay, and she isn't any different than us, right? Mom looks at me earnestly, and I say no. Julia was the one who fixed our flat tire after the funeral while Uncle Pete and Cousin Larry watched with their hands in their pockets, looking stupid.

Bobby Foley calls me "fag" all the time. I should've known it meant something like this.

6.

It's the first sunny day in March, almost warm enough to take off my coat, and it seems like everyone in the neighborhood has the same idea: baseball. Even Sally and Jill want to play, probably because the Ewing twins are all gung-ho, and Dave even asks Jill if she'll be on his team.

We all migrate to the field, and there's the eight of us: Danny and Dave Ewing, Peggy Ewing, Bobby Foley, Jill, Sally, Pinky, and me. We split into teams of four, and I'm with Dave, Jill, and Pinky. I'm glad we have Dave and not Danny; Danny hits more home runs, but Dave runs faster and catches better, so he can cover both second and third base by himself. I like to play catcher, because there's less pressure; I'm less likely to muff a play. I can throw to first and third pretty easily from there and don't have to run much to chase the balls. Plus, my dad gave me a catcher's mitt for my 11th birthday, so I'm the natural choice. The only person I'll share the glove with is Sally, so she catches for the other side, and we hand the glove off to each other between each inning. Danny Ewing brings a hockey mask, but Sally won't wear it because it messes up her hair. I wear it behind the plate. Our pitcher is Jill, and although she hasn't beaned me in the face with the ball yet, better safe than sorry.

Surprise, surprise—we're all getting along pretty much, although Bobby and I are giving each other a lot of space. Sally and Jill are flirting with the Ewing twins, though Jill remains pretty focused on the game, despite flashing her most brilliant smile at Dave every time he makes a play. By dinnertime, the other team is up by two, and we all agree that this is the last inning. Our batting line-up is Dave, Pinky, me, then Jill. Dave hits a single, then Pinky strikes out, then

I foul out, then Jill hits a single. I run out to stand in for Dave on second, and he bunts it, making it to first. Now we've got me on third for Dave, Jill on second, and Dave on first. There are two outs, and Stinky Pinky is back up at bat. I can see the sweat on her upper lip; she wipes it off with the back of her hand and taps the bat on the plate. Sure, she's nervous—I would be, too. Bases loaded, two outs, and she has to know she's the worst hitter on either team. I feel terrible for her: If she strikes out, she'll be razzed for months by the other kids in the neighborhood, more so than she already is. Just last week, Bobby Foley stole her Cabbage Patch doll and drew bushy eyebrows and a moustache on it with permanent marker. Poor Pinky cried all day after she found the doll, lying face-up in a puddle outside her house. I say a silent prayer—*please God, for her sake, let Pinky hit the ball*—and miracle of miracles, she does! Pink makes her way to first base, a stunned smile on her face, and I trot home, narrowing the gap in the score.

Uh-oh. Now *I'm* up, bases are loaded, two outs. I could win the game for us right here. Or lose it.

Time for another prayer. *Please, God, let me do this. Give me a hit, let me walk, something.* Was I just feeling sorry for Stinky Pinky a minute ago? If I screw this up, I'll get the razzing instead of her. I step up to the plate and swallow hard. *This is it, Curtis. Your chance to be a hero. Don't screw it up.*

Bobby Foley is pitching for their team, and he flashes me his meanest smile. He cocks his arm back and lets the first pitch fly. I swing. Strike one.

He must have been feeling too cocky, because he fumbles the second pitch, and the ball hits the dirt in front of home plate and bounces up. Ball one. Bobby lets loose a stream of curses, one of which I've never heard before and make note to ask Sally later what it means. Sally scoops up the misthrow and fires the ball back at Bobby.

His next pitch is low, and I swing again. It shoots out to the left of third base, flying wild. Foul ball. Strike two.

I cover my face for a moment, wiping the sweat from my forehead with my shirt. *Please, God. Please ... Nana. Nana, help me just get this one hit. For you.*

There's nothing stronger than calling on your dead grandmother to help you get a hit. I finish wiping my face, and I feel the corners of my mouth pull up, just a little. I'm going to get a hit. It's *impossible* for me to miss. Not with Nana on my side!

Bobby winds up and throws his finest fastball, sending it right over home plate. I've got this. I pull back and swing as hard as I can. Maybe Nana will give me a triple or—dare I dream it? A home run, even?

My head is full of images of Dave Ewing and Jill hoisting me on their shoulders and carrying me home, slapping me on the back and calling me a regular Reggie Jackson. It takes me a moment to register what I have not heard: the solid clunk of ball connecting with bat.

I miss.

I look back at Sally, who is beaming, the ball nestled firmly in my mitt. I look over at Dave Ewing, who is drawing a finger across his throat and then pointing at me, then at Jill, who's scowling. I missed. I just lost the game for us.

"Sorry," I mumble to Dave as he stalks past me, and he shakes his head. I don't think he even wants to talk to me right now.

I drag my feet as I head home. Sally's lingering with Jill, and I make it into the house before I cry, just a little. Sally comes in and sees me.

"Oh, Curtis, get over it. It's just a game. It's not like we're in the big leagues or anything, for chrissake."

"But I promised Nana I'd hit the ball for her," I admit, my voice catching. "I told her I'd get a hit just for her, and I didn't. I'm the worst grandson ever."

Sally looks at me for a moment and then throws her arm over my shoulder, a rare moment when I feel like we're on the same side. "Well, there you go, silly. I promised Nana *my* team would win today, just for her, and we couldn't both win for her, right? See?"

I look at Sally's bright eyes, and she winks at me. She's right; it makes perfect sense. I wish I'd known she'd done that, or I never would have prayed for Pinky to get a hit. Clearly, I need to learn to use the power of prayer a little more carefully.

Mom has made macaroni and cheese for dinner, which helps, too.

7.

I know I'm old enough to not have Sally babysit me anymore, and Sally agrees. It makes me feel like a stupid baby to have to tag along with her every day, and Sally doesn't really want me hanging out with her and Jill. She and I have teamed together to have a hundred arguments with Mom about it, but Mom is firm. I can't be left home alone until I turn twelve, which is six long months away.

Sally drags me over to Jill's house every afternoon so the two of them can talk about the boys in their class. I usually entertain myself with my comic books or by wandering down to Danny and David's house to watch them work on their matching motorbikes. Neither one has gotten his running yet, but it's going to happen any day now. They take turns stopping every twenty minutes or so to try to kick-start the ignition. Each time they do, I hold my breath, but I'm starting to suspect they might need a few more hours in shop class before anything's really going to happen.

I haven't been able to look Jill directly in the eye since I've lately realized that her boobs are just about the nicest in the world, but that doesn't mean I don't try to look down her shirt when the opportunity presents itself. Today, she's wearing a red sweater with a neck that scoops out, daring me to take a peek. She's sitting with Sally underneath the crabapple tree in front of Jill's duplex, and I am overcome with the urge to collect apples at that very moment. I scramble up the trunk, waiting for Sally to yell at me to go away, as she often does when I get too close to their endless gabbing, but she ignores me. *Captain Invisible!* I make it up to the second fork in the branch. I can't quite see down Jill's top, but I can't lean over any further without being obvious, and I can't go up any higher or the whole tree-climbing thing will be pointless.

My next thought is ingenious. If I hook my knees over the branch and hang upside down, not only will I get a clear view of Jill's cream-colored bra, but I might also impress her to boot. She'll clap and tell me I'm the best acrobat she's ever seen, and that I should drop down as fast as I can so she can give me a kiss. It's this image, of Jill leaning in to plant her thick red lips on mine, that I'm thinking of when my leg slips, and I pitch forward.

I scream as I fall, which is how Sally and Jill manage to roll out of my way as I tumble to the ground. I feel my arm snap, and I blink for a moment before I feel the hot pain shoot up to my shoulder. That's when I start to wail, not caring if Jill thinks I'm a baby. I start to shout, and the word that comes out in a stream, over and over, is *that* word, the one that makes Mom turn purple and slap your face if you say it near her.

"Fuckfuckfuckityfuckfuck!" I howl, clutching my arm and struggling to stand.

Sally checks my eyes, asks me if I'm okay, and assures me I'm not dead. I continue my cursing between tears and hiccups. Sally tells me to shut up, *fast*, and I spin around to see Mrs. Ewing. She's frowning.

"We're going to the hospital. In the car. NOW!" Mrs. Ewing barks, and Sally and I march after her, our heads down. Sally probably figures she's in for it because I broke my arm on her watch, but she's got nothing to worry about once Mrs. Ewing tells Mom how bad I cursed. I've seen steam come out of Mom's ears when she hears that word. And that was when *Dad* said it.

It's just Sally, Mrs. Ewing, and me in the car, so I cry without fear of being teased. Hot throbbing waves of pain burn up my wrist, past my elbow, and claw their way up my bicep. I'm pretty sure the doctors are going to have to amputate, and I want them to; it hurts so bad.

Mrs. Ewing brings me to Saint Peter's, the closest hospital to The Meadows. She tells Sally to run ahead and grab a wheelchair to bring me in, and she turns to me to examine my arm after I step out of the car.

"No bones poking through," she says offhandedly, gently lifting my arm to peer at my elbow. "Probably a clean fracture. You're lucky you didn't break your neck, Curtis!"

I offer her a weak smile, and then I lean forward and quietly vomit on my shoes.

"Concussion!" she shrieks, and starts pushing me toward the emergency room door, where Sally is coming out with a black metal wheelchair. "Come here with that chair and get your brother inside. He's got a concussion!"

It takes forever for the doctor to see me because they have to wait for Mom to come with her insurance card. They give me a shot of something that makes me feel happy, and Sally is suddenly coming up with her funniest lines ever. She's laughing, too, and I think for a moment she might be laughing at me, but I don't care. When Mom gets here and Mrs. Ewing tells her the swear words I used, I'm as good as dead anyway, so might as well enjoy my last few minutes with my sister the comedian. Sally crosses her eyes and snorts like a pig, and I start chuckling again.

Mom finally arrives, and a nurse wheels me in to a room, then for X-rays, then back to the room where we wait for almost an hour for a doctor to tell me I have a greenstick fracture. I guess that's a special broken bone for kids who fall out of trees. I'll need to wear a cast for six weeks. He sets my arm while I think about the next six weeks—no baseball or tree climbing, not to mention gym class. I'm going to be stuck with Albert, the fat kid with asthma, sitting along the wall in gym class, reading a biography on a famous sports figure that I'm going to have to write a book report about. This is, by far, the worst thing that's ever happened to me, and once Mom has had a chance to sit down and talk to Mrs. Ewing, I'm going to be grounded, to boot.

I look at Mom. Her mouth is turned down at the corners, and she looks like she might cry.

"How am I going to pay for this?" she whispers, almost to herself. "Insurance won't pay for much more than half. How am I going to pay?" She shakes her head.

I don't know what her problem is. I'm the one that's going to be paying—for the next six weeks.

8.

Mrs. Ewing is all right. Not only did she not tell Mom about my outburst, but she came over the day after we went to the hospital with a whole plate of those cookies with the M&Ms baked right into them. She signed my cast, too—"No Climbing! From Mrs. Ewing."

Sally is grounded for not paying attention to what I was doing, which means she can't talk on the phone or watch TV for two weeks. I can watch TV, though, and Mom makes Sally promise to sit in the kitchen while I'm in the living room watching the Creature Features that come on in the afternoon. Sally promises but comes in anyway, making fun of Mothra and Godzilla right alongside of me. She's being really nice to me, so I don't tell Mom on her. It's bad enough that Mom calls the house three or four times an afternoon. She says it's to check on me, but I think she does it to make sure Sally isn't on the phone.

The guys from The Meadows all signed my cast, and even Bobby Foley thought it was pretty cool how I did it, once I let it slip that I was trying to sneak a look down the front of Jill's shirt. We haven't gotten along this well in a long time. I picked out a biography on Bobby Orr for gym class, but I don't have to write my report right away, since I broke my right arm, which is the one I write with. I really haven't had to do much schoolwork at all lately, and I'm excused from homework until the cast comes off. I've been bored out of my mind.

Once Sally isn't grounded any more, she starts going over to Jill's after school again, but I don't have to go with her. I like to make my way down to the community center and look at the boxes to see what other people have in storage down there. I'm hoping to find Nana's boxes, to see if her stuff still smells like Jean Naté.

The inside of the community center stinks like wet cat, and there is a brown film of dust over all of the windows. There are cardboard boxes and old rocking horses, and a giant plastic tree in a lime-green pot. The boxes are arranged with no apparent rhyme or reason, and the writing is so faded on most of them, the only way to tell what's inside is to open them up and start rummaging. It's slow going, though, with one arm in a cast up to my elbow.

I find a collection of baby clothes that smell like mothballs and a box of broken Christmas ornaments. I cut my finger on one of them and suck the wound for a moment before moving the box aside and pulling up the packaging tape that seals the carton below it. The tape is warped and the stickiness is long gone, so the box opens easily. I find loose stuffing and mouse turds inside, along with what was once someone's stuffed animal collection. I slowly take the toys out, one by one, and smack the dolls' bellies and bears' heads against the box to get rid of some of the dirt that has settled there. I pick up what appears to be a small stuffed rat by the tail. Its eyes are chewed away, and its muzzle is frozen in a snarl. Realizing with a start that it's really real, and dead, I throw it at the far wall with one jerk, letting out a yelp.

"Jeez Louise! Watch it!" Stinky Pinky stands up from behind a wall of crates. She dusts off her rear and steps out from her hiding spot.

"Where did you come from? How long have you been back there?" I ask. I'm angry. I've already decided that this is *my* new secret place.

"Calm down, Curtis. I was here first," she says, jutting out her birthmarked chin and putting her hands on her hips defiantly. "I come here 'most every day, whenever you guys won't hang out with me. I've already been through all these boxes," she adds with a wave of her hand. "What are you looking for, 'zactly? I can probably tell you where it is."

I'm not about to tell Stinky Pinky I'm looking for my Nana's clothes to see if they still smell like her. She'll think I'm either a baby or a perv. Instead I shrug.

"Just looking, I guess." I hold up my cast and offer a smile. "Can't do much else these days."

Pinky nods like she knows what I mean, though I can't ever remember *her* being in a cast. She breaks out in a grin, too, and for a moment, I think she looks kind of cute. Her hair is long and clean, and she's starting to get boobs. If it weren't for that stupid raspberry on her neck and chin, I realize, she'd be good-looking.

"Want to know a secret?" she asks, looking around to make sure we're alone, although I can't imagine why any of the neighborhood gang would ever want to step in here if they didn't have to. I nod. Pinky's eyes glow, and she takes me by my good arm. "Come look over here. You won't believe what I found."

Pinky leads me to a corner with two windows, catty-corner to each other, and a tower of boxes in between. She hefts up one carton, then the next, until she gets to the third one down. She opens the lid, and I peer in. A pile of comic books look back at me, and my heart leaps. Pinky has found the mother lode! For a moment, I want to hug her, but when she looks sideways at me and frowns, I restrain myself. My fingers are itching to go through the stack, though. I can see Spider-Man dodging the Green Goblin on the top cover.

"Not those, dummy," she says, and picks up a stack of comics, tossing them to the side. The magazines below are wider and thicker, and Pinky picks one up, showing me the front.

"*These*," she whispers, giggling.

I am staring at a naked woman with boobs the size of beach balls. "Busty Heart Bares All!" it reads above her picture, but I only take a second to read the headline before I snatch it out of Pinky's hands.

"Nuh-uh," I say, awed by my very first sight of a naked girl's breasts. I fan the magazine open and am treated to my very first female crotch shot. I stop for a moment, holding my breath. There it is. That's what they've been hiding under their panties all this time.

That doesn't look like cotton candy at all.

Nana used to tell me she'd better not catch me trying to look at the girls' sweet treats, and I guess I always thought she meant that literally. Each time I tried to picture a girl naked, I imagined her with a giant pillow of cotton candy between her legs. It even made sense, in a way—when Jill was pissed, her favorite thing to hiss was a scornful "eat me!" as she flounced away. I never imagined she was referring to—well, to *that*.

The thought of Jill excites me, and I start to flip through the pages again to see if there are any black girls in the magazine. Pinky is right next to me, looking over my shoulder. I am suddenly aware that she is breathing heavily.

"Pretty gross, right?" she says with a nervous laugh, and I glare at her. I move away a little so I can keep flipping without her seeing what I'm looking for. Finally, I find it—a lanky woman with dark mocha skin. Her nipples are darker than her skin, and she's looking at the camera with her lids half closed, her legs spread. Her hand is down between her legs, exposing herself.

Wait a minute. What is that she's doing?

I look up for a moment to ponder this, and Pinky clears her throat. "Curtis? Are you okay?"

I've never been better, but I finally remember that Pinky is here with me, sharing this moment as I stare at all the nakedness I could ever want to see. My dick twitches in my jeans, and I start to feel uncomfortable. The community center is hot as a furnace all of a sudden.

"M'okay," I stutter, and Pinky moves closer.

"Curtis?" she breathes. "Do you want to kiss me?"

Suddenly, more than anything in the world, yes, I want to kiss Stinky Pinky. *Allison*, I mentally scold myself. I want to kiss Allison. I turn to face her and nod, unable to say anything, afraid of doing something stupid like spitting when I talk. She leans in, and I lean in, and at the last moment, as our lips meet, I bring my good hand up to cup her chin. Our eyes close and I think, *Why, her birthmark doesn't feel any different than the rest of her; isn't that something?*

Our kiss is wet and sloppy, and I'm not sure I like it. Allison pulls back and giggles, and I look down at my shoes, my black sneakers that Mom picked up on blue-light special a couple of months ago. "That was my first kiss," she says, trying not to smile, and I break out in to a wide grin.

"Mine too," I admit sheepishly.

"Want to do it again?" she asks, and I move in again without bothering to answer.

"I see you two! I see you!"

Bobby Foley is suddenly at the window, banging on the pane and making it shudder with his force. "You two are DEAD! I'm gonna tell! You two are doin' it and I'm gonna tell!"

Allison and I both look at the window where Bobby's face is pressed up in an angry sneer. He disappears, and Allison bursts into tears and runs out of the community center. I don't know what she's crying about. I was just caught kissing Stinky Pinky. You can't get much lower on the social scale than that.

9.

Bobby Foley is true to his word. Everyone in the neighborhood knows that Stinky Pinky and I were fooling around, and now even my own sister doesn't want to be seen in public with me. The guys at school are merciless, asking me if she's got birthmarks down *there* and leaving crude drawings of dicks and tits in my backpack. Stinky Pinky and I can't possibly sit at the same table at lunch anymore, so I start to eat alone, at my own solitary table at the farthest corner of the cafeteria. I am a total loser.

I don't know how Stinky Pinky is weathering all this, and I don't care. She tricked me into kissing her, and she wanted us to get caught. Every day when I see her, a ball of anger sits in my chest, and I want to punch her right between her pathetic puppy-dog eyes. This is all her fault.

Of course my mother had to hear about it too, which meant an absolutely mortifying talk at the kitchen table. Mom was not sympathetic to my plight at all, telling me that if I dare to stick my penis where it shouldn't go, it will burn up and fall off unless I'm married to the person I'm pointing it at. God *knows* these things. He will send His wrath down against me and charbroil my dick.

The worst part is how Jill looks at me these days. The first time I saw her after this whole catastrophe, she wrinkled up her nose at me like she smelled a fart and turned away. I want to tell her it was all a mistake. I want to tell her that I really wanted to be kissing her, not Pinky.

Life is pretty boring now that nobody will be caught dead speaking to me. Except for Asthmatic Albert, of course. Now that I'm lower than even him on the social scale, all of a sudden he thinks we're best friends. He keeps asking me how I like my Bobby Orr biography and how many pages I think my book report is going to turn out to be and if I'm a big Bruins fan because sometimes his Uncle Roy can get tickets and they drive down to Boston for the weekend and catch a game. I try to ignore him, or shut him up with a withering glance, but the truth is, when nobody will talk to you, you start to miss the company of other people. I admit to Albert that I've never seen a hockey game in person and maybe, if his uncle can get an extra ticket for free and I'm not busy, we can go to a hockey match together. Maybe. And perhaps I'll mention to him that when your name's Albert, you should try just a little harder not to be fat. But really, he's mostly just pudgy, and after all, he's the only kid who talks to me. Will it really make that much of a difference to my reputation if I'm hanging out with Fat Albert?

Since I can't play sports, and nobody would want me on their team even if I could, I hang out at the library more. At first, I pick up books about sports, but after a while, it starts to sound like the same old thing. All of the athletes I read about were really good ever since they picked up a bat and ball, or they trained themselves to get better, something that I've never experienced. I've always been average at every sport I've tried. Nobody has ever watched me kick a soccer ball or shoot a hoop and said they saw a spark of talent there. I abandon my sports biographies and start to look for other books to read.

The school library has a lot of stupid books, like the Hardy Boys and Encyclopedia Brown. I beg my Mom to let me get off the bus at the town library after school. After a few weeks of my whining, she gives in and agrees to pick me up there on her way home from work. After all, I can't get a girl pregnant at the library, right? There isn't a girl within fifty miles of Osprey Falls that wants to hold my hand, I want to tell her, but my mother isn't the most rational person these days. She doesn't understand how kissing Stinky Pinky was the kiss of death for me. She warns me not to get in any trouble, or I'll be coming to work with her and washing the floors at K-Mart after school.

The town library is huge. It looks like a mansion of gray brick on the outside, with cobblestone paths and benches that go all the way around the outside of the building. I get lost in the stacks the first day and end up sitting in an aisle, staring at a huge book with a guy in white battling swords with a dark, beaked figure on the cover. The dark man is wearing funny slippers that end in a point, almost like a hooked claw. I pick it up and start to read. My whole world becomes about *The Stand*, a massive battle between good and evil, and I just know I'd be at Hemingford Home with the good guys, never having to bother with Bobby Foley ever again, as he would naturally be right in Vegas with the devil. I can't stop reading it. I finish it in a week and want to start again, but I find some other books by the same author, and soon I have devoured *The Shining*, and *Carrie*, and *Cujo*.

"Big fan of horror, huh?" the ancient librarian says to me when I lay down my armful on the counter, and now I have a word for it. *Horror*. Now I know what section to look for when I come to the library every day.

My afternoons are filled with werewolves and demons and girls with psychic abilities that they use on the mean people at school. My best friends are guys like Stephen King and Jack Ketchum and Peter Straub, men I've never met but who get it, get how horrible and mean the world can be. I pick up a copy of *Off Season* for a quarter at the library book sale and lend it to Albert when I'm done, and soon he's at the library next to me, as we flip through the pages together, pausing from time to time to talk about how awesome it would be to be a vampire or have telekinesis. We experiment with trying to move books with just our mind or set the library's copier on fire with our eyes. There's a whole world of otherworldly things out there. We get to peek in to it when we read these books, but we haven't been able to quite find it in our lives, yet. I think about Bobby Foley and the guys who left the dirty pictures in my backpack and how nice it would be to be able to set them on fire with just a glare. If only. If only.

10.

For my twelfth birthday, I tell Mom I want to go to the movies. She tells me I can invite one friend, which is good, because I only have one friend who would even consider coming with me. Albert's mom drops him off at the Showcase in East Bailey right at 4 p.m., and I meet him out front. Mom seems a little hurt when I tell her I don't want her coming into the theater with us and watching the movie, but come on. I'm twelve now. I'm practically a teenager.

We tell Mom we're going to the 4:45 showing of *The Transformers: The Movie*. It's rated PG, so she's fine with that, and she tells me she'll be back to pick us up at 6:30. *Transformers* was actually a compromise with Mom. I wanted to see *Stand by Me*, but when Mom found out it there was a dead body involved, she immediately vetoed it. She countered with *Howard the Duck*, which sounded so unbelievably stupid I asked her if she thought I was retarded. Then she told me if I kept up my attitude, I'd be spending my birthday in my room, reorganizing my closet. So *Transformers* it is.

Al and I wait in line for our tickets. We're discussing an important new development at school, namely, Wanda Wilkes is getting boobs. She's not wearing a training bra yet, but she probably should be. Al tells me that he could see her nipples right through the white T-shirt she was wearing on Friday. I'm pissed that I didn't notice.

Two kids behind us mention the *Transformers* movie. They've clearly already seen it and start talking about the big war over planet Cybertron, and how Optimus Prime and Starscream die. One kid mentions that when Unicron reformats Megatron into Galvatron, it's so cool that Mr. Spock from *Star Trek* is his voice. I turn around to yell at them for spoiling all the major plot points for those of us that haven't seen it yet, and see that the kids are nine years old at best.

"Uh-oh," I whisper to Al. "I think this movie might be totally gay."

Al nods, but it's too late. We're at the counter, and there's nothing to do but buy our tickets. We do, and after hitting the concession stand for Sour Patch Kids and soda, we head toward theater number three, resigned to our fate. We'll go see this stupid kiddie movie, but neither of us will ever admit to anyone we know that we did.

Al nudges me as we trudge toward the doorway to *Transformers*. Just past our entrance is theater number four, which clearly reads *Friday the 13th Part VI: Jason Lives*, 4:35. He doesn't have to say anything. I nod, and we keep on walking. My heart is in my throat, and I can't help but look back as we turn left into the forbidden R-rated movie to see if anyone's chasing after us. I imagine an usher running down the purple-carpeted hallway, ready to snatch us by the backs of our shirts and call the cops to report our felony.

Nobody comes. We sneak in and find two seats toward the back, trying to look as normal and casual as possible. We slide down into our seats, scrunching down, attempting to make ourselves as small and invisible as we can. Now the real terror starts. We just have to make it to the start of the movie, when the lights go dark, before we'll truly be safe.

Amazingly, the people filtering in to find seats don't look our way at all. It's 4:32, according to the Timex Mom gave me for my birthday. Just a few minutes more.

My stomach lurches when a short, balding man with tattoos starts climbing the stairs toward the back seats where Al and I are pretending to be invisible. His gold chains reflect in the runner lights, and my heart sinks. It's our neighbor, Mr. Jervis. I'm dead. My mother will never let me out of the house again.

I keep my eyes on the blank screen, determined not to make eye contact. If I don't look at him, maybe he won't recognize me. What the heck is he doing here anyway? The man rarely leaves his side of the duplex, except to occasionally shoot squirrels on the lawn or smoke a cigar outside if the weather's nice. Did Mom send him to follow me? Did she know all along that I might try to pull something like this, now that I'm twelve? My dread grows as he gets closer and closer. She *knew*. She knew she couldn't trust me, and she's probably been talking to Mr. Jervis about this all along, how this day would come, how her son would disappoint her by sneaking in to an R-rated movie, and how he'd have to be there to catch me, stop me before I corrupt myself to the point where I can't be saved.

Mr. Jervis stops, two rows in front of us, and takes a seat near the aisle. He never even looks up at where Al and I are cowering. I breathe a sigh of relief. Happy birthday to me!

The movie opens with someone digging up a grave, and this big, hulking guy in a hockey mask punching someone's heart out. The guy in the mask, Jason Voorhees, then goes on to stab some camp counselors with a fence post, decapitate a few people, rip one guy's arm off, dismember someone with a machete, and kill one man with a dart to the forehead. It is without a doubt the best movie I've ever seen.

When Mom meets us in front of the theater later, I feel a little guilty as we slide into the back seat.

"How was it?" Mom asks, and Al tells her about the big war over planet Cybertron, and how Optimus Prime and Starscream die. He mentions how it was pretty cool, because when Megatron is reborn as Galvatron, Spock from *Star Trek* does his voice. Mom seems to be satisfied, and we stop at Baskin Robbins for ice cream before dropping Al off at his house. I can't wait to see him on Monday so we can talk about this amazing thing, the forbidden world of R-rated movies.

All in all, it's my best birthday so far.

11.

I'm lying in my closet, thinking about the dream I just had about Jill. She was in her bikini, and she was licking the face of the keyboardist from Duran Duran. He was reaching around her back to untie her top when he turned to me and said "Curtis, why don't you come here?" So I joined in and got to feel Jill's beautiful tits, touch her hard nipples, and she reached over to rub my belly ... and that's when I woke up, shooting jizz all over my sheets.

I know immediately what's happened. It's pitch black, and I've just had a wet dream, and now, as punishment, I am blind.

How in the hell am I going to explain to my mother that I went blind coming in a dream?

A few more blinks and I can make out a faint line of light underneath my closet door. Not blind. That's a relief. Wait. The keyboardist from Duran Duran had a major supporting role in my first erotic dream. Am I gay?

I ball up my sheets in a corner. I'm going to try to wash them when I get home without Sally noticing. She's usually in charge of the laundry, but I'm sure she won't mind if I offer to do it instead.

I'm so preoccupied all day with getting those sheets and my pajamas washed that I flub a question about our assigned reading when Mrs. Downs calls on me. It's agonizing to sit through an hour of MTV, and I can't look Jill in the eye, not that she notices. When "Hungry Like the Wolf" comes on, I get up to go to the bathroom. I can't look at that guy. I study my dick in the bathroom, but I don't see any open sores or signs that it has now, officially, shot its first load. I rub it a little, and it gets hard again, and, what the hell, I can take a few minutes in here. I close my eyes and picture Jill's tits from last night, and before you know it, I'm coming in her toilet. I'm pretty sure I am officially a pervert.

When we finally get back to our house, I run up the stairs to my closet and slide the door open.

My sheets are gone.

I look around for a moment, wondering if I misplaced them. I shuffle through my boxes. I was out of sorts this morning; maybe I stuffed them somewhere to hide them better and forgot.

The sheets are definitely missing.

I find them in the dryer, which means Mom found them. I'm scared and a little bit relieved, because now I can ask her if she thinks I'm gay. I don't want Sally to hear me, though, so I sit by the front door, pretending to read a stack of Batman comics, waiting to get to Mom first. Sally, as usual, ignores me, and, for once, I am grateful. Pay no heed to the kid with the comics in the corner. Continue to paint your nails and call Jack Robertson in the eleventh grade and giggle and hang up when he answers. I am amazed at how easy it is for me to disappear in to the background. This could be handy, my ability to disappear. I feel like I've discovered a new superpower. I look up from the *Batman Special #1* that I've re-read four times in the past hour and make a face at Sally. Nothing.

I can't believe I've wasted so much time trying to sneak around her. I'm pretty sure I could march right out in to the backyard when she and Jill are tanning and stare right down the front of Jill's top and neither one would notice. The possibilities dance in front of my eyes. There are cookies to be swiped, diaries to be read …

Mom's key in the door shakes me from my daydreaming. She sees me in the corner and smiles. So I'm not invisible to everyone, then.

"Sally, hon? Can you run over to Jill's and ask her mother if she has some celery I can borrow? I need it for dinner."

Great. Now dinner won't be for an hour, because Sally can't ever make a short trip out of running over to Jill's. Doesn't Mom know that?

Mom says, "I want to talk to you for a minute, Curtis."

Wait … what? Can't we just have a quick *"I washed your sheets, Curtis. Anything you want to ask me?"* kind of moment?

Sally leaps up and skips out the door to visit Jill, and I shuffle to the kitchen table, where all the big talks happen. Am I in trouble? I would've washed the sheets myself. Quite frankly, I would've *preferred* that, but Mom apparently had one of her manic cleaning moments and decided today was the day to scour the house from top to bottom, including my closet with its terrible, jizz-soaked secret.

Mom sits down across from me and smiles. Like this is a proud moment. That's kind of sick.

What comes next is almost worse than cancer. Mom proceeds to tell me that all young men have wet dreams, and that it's perfectly normal. She says that I shouldn't be embarrassed about it, and it just means that I've officially hit puberty, when a young boy starts to turn into a man. Soon I'll start growing hair in my armpits and my crotch, and before you know it, I'll be shaving, too. I might be noticing that the girls in my class are developing breasts and looking a lot prettier to me than they used to. She tells me it's okay to look, but if she ever catches me doing anything more than that, she'll cut off my hands and burn them in the oven. Like when I was kissing Stinky Pinky. None of that nonsense will be tolerated in Mom's house.

Then she tells me I might sometimes get the urge to touch my penis, which is perfectly normal, too. My face reddens when I think about this afternoon in Jill's bathroom. *Happening sooner than you think, Ma.* She says she knows it's difficult with Sally and I sharing the same room, but maybe I could go in to the bathroom if I get that urge, because that's a private thing to do, and it should be done in a room with a door that locks. *Aha! I'm a genius!*

And if I have any more questions about it, I can always talk to my dad, or to Mr. Jervis next door. Is she crazy? The same guy that likes to rev his engine and swerve his Scout when he sees me on the sidewalk, pretending he's gonna hit me? No thanks. Then she pulls out a stick of deodorant that she picked up at work for me and tells me I'll probably want to start using it soon, especially after gym class. Like I haven't been secretly using her deodorant for at least a year now. At least I won't smell like baby powder any more. I pop it open and give it a sniff. Old Spice. Nice. Mom finishes up by saying that she hopes I'll be able to talk to her and not be ashamed if I soil my sheets again, and asking me to let her know if I'd prefer boxers or briefs the next time I need more underwear.

I want to die. I really want my mother to stop talking to me about my penis. I ask her nervously if I can have five minutes to call Dad. She nods, a little gratefully, I suspect, and I dial Dad's number.

"What's up, boy?" Dad says. Distracted.

"Um, Dad, just a quick question. I had a—er—dream last night, and, uh, there was a guy in it."

"What kind of dream?" Dad says, more interested now.

"Um, you know. A sexy-type dream. Do you think I might be queer?"

"Did he suck your dick, Curtis?"

"Oh, gross, Dad. No! There was a girl in there, too. I just, you know … messed around with her."

"And there was absolutely no cock sucking on either of your parts? Are you sure?"

"Yeah, Dad, I'm sure. But he was there. It was one of the guys in Duran Duran."

"Those pretty boys? I think you're fine, Curtis. Christ, they wear more makeup than your mother. I wouldn't worry about it. Nobody's tried to suck your dick, though, right? You just tell them no if anyone asks, you hear me?"

Well, that was humiliating. After assuring him that no old perverts have asked to see the goods, I get off the phone.

It is Sally, ironically, who puts my fears to rest once and for all. I find an opportunity over dinner to comment on how all of the guys in Duran Duran look like they're gay, she heatedly informs me that all of them are, in fact, married. To women. Which is a huge relief. If the guy popping up in my wet dream isn't gay, then hell, I must not be, either.

12.

It's a sunny day, and I'm spending it in my favorite place: the library. Al isn't here today. He's been sick for the last couple of days. It works out fine; bullies like Bobby Foley don't hang out around books, so I usually feel pretty safe among the stacks. I'm almost through *Flesh* by Richard Laymon, and I want to finish it here, because Mom's picking me up on the way home from work, and I think she might flip if she sees the title of this book. It's about cannibalism, not sex, but Mom probably wouldn't entirely believe me if I told her that. I've been reading it in segments each afternoon that I can get here, and I'm sure I just need about one more hour to wrap it up.

The librarians all know me, so none of them even look up when I take the book outside to one of the benches. There's a stone wall between the benches and the library lawn, and anyone hanging out on the grass would have to look hard to even notice someone sitting outside. I hunker down with my cannibals, totally entranced, and don't even hear the group of guys on the library lawn until I hear my sister's name.

"Sally Price? Sure, I've seen her tits. Who hasn't?"

I lift my head up slowly, trying to see who's talking without letting them know I'm here. I can see Jack Robertson, Tom Webber, and Rusty Graves, standing by the big oak that according to the plaque in front of it was planted "in memory of Marine Sargent David Coullard." They're smoking, not twenty feet away from me. I panic. I slowly slide off the bench and squat next to the stone wall, hoping to hear them better.

"You saw her tits? Shit, she gave me a hummer behind the Whole Donut," Rusty laughs, and I gulp. I have a good idea of what a hummer is, thanks to the extensive sex education I've been getting on the school bus ever since Bobby Foley got a blowjob from Wanda Wilkes and described it in great detail to everyone within earshot. It's pretty disgusting to think about my sister doing that, and my ears go hot in anger. I have the sudden, crazy urge to stand up and call all of them liars, but they're in the eleventh grade and could easily beat the crap out of me. Out of self-preservation, I stay still, but I'm furious that these assholes are talking about my big sister that way. They quickly move on to Elaine Jessop, who, according to Tom, is "like a doorknob. Everybody gets a turn." I wait, listening to them talk, until I hear their voices fade. I peek over the wall to confirm they're making their way down the sidewalk toward the pharmacy and jump up to get back inside the library. I remember to retrieve my book from the bench—no matter how pissed off I am, the desk clerk will yell at me if I leave library property outside where it might get damaged. I put it back on the shelf and simmer in the sci-fi section, thinking about what I just heard. I'm too steamed to read, so I slowly plot out the deaths of Jack Robertson, Tom Webber, and Rusty Graves. I decide on a particularly painful and gruesome fate for Rusty—skinning him alive, listening to him scream as I peel his face off with an X-Acto knife. Nobody talks about Sally like that and gets away with it. I wait for Mom, pacing, frustrated at my powerlessness. Wait until I'm older. I'll get them.

Back at the house, I try to avoid Sally, but it's a small house, so it's kind of hard. She's her usual self, telling Mom over dinner about her history teacher, Mr. Durden. They're learning about the Vietnam War, and Mr. Durden says that if President Kennedy lived, it never would've happened, and does Mom agree?

Mom sighs, says we'll never know, and Sally continues on about how good-looking Kennedy was, and did Mom think he was hot? Because, Sally adds, he was pretty hot.

Mom rolls her eyes and starts clearing away the plates. Usually one of us does it, and since Sally set the table for dinner, it really should be me cleaning it up, but I let Mom. I try to study Sally out of the corner of my eye to see if she's giving off any signals that she might have given Rusty Graves a blowjob behind the Whole Donut. She doesn't look any different to me.

After dinner, Mom and I watch TV while Sally gets on the phone. She and Jill are talking about guys, I think, and I try to tune in to her conversation to see if she mentions any of the butt wipes that were at the library today. Unfortunately, because of the close proximity of our mother, Sally often drops down to a whisper, so I don't hear much, except that I'm pretty sure both she and Jill think Mr. Wild, their sociology teacher, is hot. Jesus, the way she talks, no wonder she's getting a reputation. Who the hell *doesn't* she think is hot? And President Kennedy and Mr. Wild? What's with all the old men?

Later on, before bed, Sally and I are alone in our room. She's sitting on her bed, painting her toenails, and I'm in my closet, door open, watching her.

"I saw some guys at the library today," I start, unable to contain my curiosity.

"Oh yeah? Anybody good?" she asks, concentrating on her toes.

"Tom Webber, Jack Robertson, and Rusty Graves," I say, trying to sound casual. "Do you know them?" Which is stupid, because I know she had a huge crush on Jack last year.

"Yeah, I know them. They're all assholes. Want to hear a secret? Don't tell Mom, though." Uh oh. *Do* I want to hear a secret?

"Sure," I say, scratching my arm, pretending like I'm not dying to hear what she has to say. "What?"

"Jack offered me twenty dollars to flash him. You know," she explains, looking up from her pedicure, "to show him my boobs. I told him to fuck off."

"What a jerkoff," I laugh, relieved.

"I know, right?" Sally says, smiling and finishes painting her toenails. I tell her good night and close my closet door.

She told him to fuck off. I *knew* my sister wasn't a slut. They were probably talking bad about her just because she wouldn't give them the time of day. Assholes.

13.

I start high school today. My cast is long gone, but still I am not picked for kickball teams or volleyball. I am ignored; my sin with Pinky is sticking to me like a cloud of leprosy. High school is huge, and kids from four different middle schools around town go there, but it's like they all know. There is an unspoken stigma that hangs around me, and I can't seem to shake it. Albert is still my only friend, and he and I sit at lunch together at a small table, drawing our own comic books in which we star as massively muscled werewolves that save the girl and kill the Bobby Foleys of the world. I did make one last trip to the community center and snatched up the comic books Pinky had so carelessly tossed aside; I might have grabbed a few of the nudie magazines, too. Both are fascinating to Albert and me.

I have English class with Marcy Middleton, the most beautiful girl in ninth grade. She has emerald green eyes that are always smiling, and curly red hair that makes me long to reach out and pull on a soft curl, just to see it bounce back. She's nice to everyone and is never embarrassed to answer a question in class, even if her answer is wrong. Marcy beams at everyone when she walks down the hall, even me. I think I'm in love.

I think about Marcy when I'm safe in my closet. Sally works at the doughnut shop in town now, so when I come home from school, if I'm not at the library or at Albert's house, I go right in my closet and think about Marcy and jerk off. Jill is a figment of my past, a girl I once liked in a vague sort of way. Marcy is a woman.

Albert's family has some money, which I didn't realize until the first time I went over to his house. When he opened the door, the first thing that struck me was how white everything was. The walls were bright and spotless, and even the hallway from the door to the kitchen was carpeted in plush beige. His house smells like cinnamon and apples, and you can't tell a kid lives there at all.

Albert doesn't fit in even in his own home. His kitchen is all smooth metal and polished, and he just stands there, wheezing and sweating from the exertion of coming home. He's still fat, and his polo shirts and pressed khakis are always a little too tight, so that his shirt rides up and his belly peeks out. He's starting to get a lot of zits, too, which isn't making him any more popular than he is now. I can smell him before I see him sometimes, because it seems like he's always red and sweating. At least I match my home. Our duplex is always shabby and a little bit dusty, just like me. With my K-Mart clothes and shaggy hair that I can never seem to get to sit right, I fit in to my side of town perfectly. I would rather die than have Albert over to my house.

When we hang out, we pretend to be monsters and warlocks, devils and superheroes. Albert's got a huge collection of X-Men comic books, and we read through them and pretend we're Wolverine and Gambit, acting them out and of course, always getting the girl. Albert is always Wolverine and winds up with Rogue more often than not in his fantasy. My Gambit always winds up with Marcy Middleton.

Whenever a new Stephen King or Dean Koontz book comes out, Albert has his mother pick up a copy for him, and he lets me read it as soon as he's done, so we've both pored over the pages before it even gets in at the library. Then we talk about how cool it would be to be psychically connected to a homicidal maniac or whether there's a possibility that the pet cemetery behind the vet's office has the ability to bring animals and people back from the dead.

For a fat, asthmatic goofball, Albert has turned out to be okay.

Sally works four days a week at the Whole Donut. She never brings home any extras. Sometimes after work she goes out with Derek Lombardo, a skinny guy she works with who has his own car. Derek drives a lumbering brown Dodge Dart, which looks like a giant turd parked outside our house when he drops her off. Mom must not have had the whole "your private parts will be charbroiled" speech with Sally, because I've walked by that Dart a few times, and it's been rocking, and the windows are steamed up. Albert says he's heard my sister is a slut. I punched him hard in the arm when he told me that, even though, at this point, I'm pretty sure it's true. But she's still my sister, and I don't want Albert talking about her that way.

All of the girls from The Meadows seem to have a reputation for being easy these days, and it's too much for me to argue on behalf of my sister's honor. Even Stinky Pinky is in on it, wearing tank tops with no bra to school and flirting with the guys who take wood shop. Jill dropped out this fall, and I heard Sally whispering to Derek that Jill is pregnant. One of the Ewing twins is supposedly the father.

If the girls from The Meadows are easy, the guys are dangerous. The Ewing brothers turned in their mopeds for motorcycles, and you can hear them buzzing through the neighborhood at all hours of the night, laughing and hollering. Bobby Foley must be working out, because he's got muscles now and plays on the junior varsity football team. His head is shaved, and he wears white wife-beater tanks all the time. He doesn't bother to acknowledge my existence, except to occasionally spit in my general direction if he's got a clear trajectory in the hallway. Sometimes he spits straight up in the air and catches it in his mouth again. I know he thinks this is cool, but I watched Marcy Middleton one day as she saw him do it, and she grimaced and shook her head like she'd bitten into a lemon. She must think it's gross, so I stopped practicing it in the bathroom at home.

I don't seem to have a dangerous reputation. Albert says I'm cultivating the quiet, brooding look, which is his way of saying I'm a loser. None of the girls flirt with me or talk to me. Mom has nothing to worry about, because I'm not getting laid any time soon.

Only Marcy seems to notice me as I slink down the hallway between classes, as close to the wall as possible. She always smiles at me. Just last week, after English class, Marcy said "bye" to me as we walked out the classroom. And right across the way, staring at me with slitted, angry eyes, was Bobby Foley.

14.

We have career day at school, which I think is a little ridiculous since I'm barely fifteen, but Mom says you can never decide on a future too soon, and I can always change my mind later. There are about twenty different people to go listen to, but we're only allowed to pick three. Albert and I sign up for the farmer, because Albert thinks he might want to be a cowboy someday; the teacher, because it's Mr. Wild, and he's funny; and the paramedic, because he's scheduled for right after lunch and we can get out of school early if we've already been to three people by sixth period.

The farmer talks about his day, how he gets up at 4:30 to milk cows and feed the calves. Albert asks him if he has any horses on the farm and does he use them to round up the cattle, but the guy says no, chasing the cows on horseback scares the milk out of them. I'm not sure if the farmer is serious or not, but farming sounds like a lot of hard work, and I just don't think I'm ambitious enough. Mr. Wild's presentation is a little better, talking about how much fun it is to mold young minds, plus he can instill a love for Peter Frampton into each and every one of us. I don't see myself as a teacher, though. I don't think I'd have the patience to be nice to the Bobby Foleys in my classroom.

It's the paramedic that catches my attention. He's wearing a uniform with EMS on the sleeve, and I remember the man who was so nice to me the day I found Nana. He talks about riding in ambulances and saving lives and how exciting and sad and amazing his job is. There's only one mantra in our house these days, so I ask him: "Do you have to go to school for that? I mean, how much does it cost to become a paramedic?"

He explains that you have to become an EMT first, and do your ride time and get a little more comfortable with the profession before you even think about going to paramedic school, which can cost more than $2,000. But EMT school is about $800.

I decide to start right away on my new career. I can start saving now, I figure, if I can find a part-time job. After school, I stop in every place I could think of downtown, but neither the library, the pharmacy, the low-fat yogurt shop, nor the deli is hiring. I trudge back to The Meadows, head down low, when I realize I'm passing the old folks' home where Nana sometimes went to visit her friend Bee Bee. *Who does the laundry and the cooking and the dishes there?* I wonder. These are all chores I did at Nana's and still do at home, so it's not like they'd have to train me. It's close to home, kind of related to the emergency medical services field, and worth a shot, so I shuffle up the front walk, eyeing a man in a red shirt and white trousers that match his thick white hair, who is beaming and waving at every car that drives by.

I open the main door and find myself in a cream-colored hallway. There isn't a soul in sight. I can smell the vague scent of the pine cleaner that my mother uses when she cleans the floors. There's another odor hiding underneath—the paramedic smelled like this, too.

I start my slow walk down the hallway, and, eventually, it opens up to a broad room with a high ceiling and windows in the roof to let the light in. There's a desk with a frowning woman behind it. She's got a phone to her left ear, and she's writing on graph paper with her right hand. She looks up at me from beneath brassy red bangs, holds up a finger to let me know she's going to be a minute, and tells the person on the phone that she has promised her colleagues a band for Memorial Day, and by golly, they had better deliver her one. She has a large population of veterans among her colleagues, and if the Cheshire County Bugle Boys can't show her people the respect they deserve for putting their lives on the line for this great nation, not only will she find a band that can, she will make sure the newspaper and the TV reporters and every other media person she can think of will hear about the shabby treatment the Bugle Boys gave her veterans. The woman slams down the phone and wipes her hand down the front of her blouse, as if the whole phone call has left her stained.

"Hello there," she finally says to me, and I'm relieved to see she's smiling. "How can I help you today?"

For a moment, I have no voice, but finally I clear my throat and answer. "I'm looking for a job," I say in a voice just a hair above a whisper. I cough and try again. "My name is Curtis Price, and I'm looking for a job," I say, stronger, louder. "You don't happen to have any?"

Her name is Dottie and, as a matter of fact, they're looking for someone to help with general cleaning in the afternoons. "But I can't just hand it out willy-nilly," she says. "Are you qualified to work in a convalescent home?"

The truth is, I'm probably not, but I try to play it cool and shrug. "I help my Mom with cleaning all the time. I bet I can handle it," I answer.

"That's fine if you're applying for a job as a housekeeper in a hotel," Dottie says, the sides of her mouth turning downward. "But my colleagues here are special people. We like to make sure our employees are the kind of people who will take the time to listen to them when they're telling a story and actually hear what they're saying. That they'll be patient if one of our ladies is taking her time walking down the hall, blocking the path with her walker. That they'll treat our folks with the dignity and respect they deserve, even when they're throwing out an adult diaper or washing sheets that might have been soiled. Is that something you think you can do, Curtis?"

I look at her, and, all of a sudden, I want to cry. "I was very close with my Nana," I say, my voice catching. "I would have done all those things for her. We used to play Scrabble together, and she'd tell me stories about my Pop-Pop. I miss her," I add, and Dottie looks at me for a long moment.

"I'm sure you do. I think you'll work out fine," she says gently and pats me on the shoulder. "Come back tomorrow at 3:30, and I'll show you the ropes."

I have a job! I leave Sunny Brook Convalescent Home with a smile on my face, and I even wave bravely to Mr. Whitepants as I skip down the front walk. "See you tomorrow!" I call out, and he beams at me, waving.

Dottie is waiting for me when I arrive ten minutes early the next day. "Prompt, Curtis. I like that," she says with a nod and shows me where the closet is with the cleaning supplies. "Your job is going to be to wipe down the rooms, strip the beds, and sweep and wash the floors," she tells me. "If someone wants to talk to you a bit, sit down and talk to them. I'm more concerned that you'll treat our tenants with kindness than with the number of rooms you clean in a day. I don't want you pretending like our colleagues aren't there. Nobody likes to feel like they just blend in with the wallpaper."

I study Dottie's face carefully. Is she talking about me? I have perfected the art of blending in to the background. Can she tell? I want to tell her that it's not such a bad place to be, but I hold my tongue.

I start to make my rounds, and I know I'm going slowly, but I'm not really sure if I'm doing it right. I dust the end tables and windowsills of Mrs. Cotter's room, and she tells me she has three granddaughters about my age. I look at the picture on her nightstand as I dust the frame, and her grandchildren look like they're half my age, but I don't correct her. I stop and smile shyly at her and let her tell me about Gabby, who takes ballet lessons and will dance with Baryshnikov someday, and Jenny, who is in the fourth grade and already paints like Picasso, and Hope, who is the family nature girl, and is always bringing dried flowers and pressed leaves and the occasional frog when she comes to visit Mrs. Cotter. I realize that I don't need to say much of anything when I'm talking to Mrs. Cotter, or Ms. Graves, or Mr. Peterson. They will do all the talking. I just have to hear them.

By the end of my shift, I have met only seven of the residents at Sunny Brook, but Dottie tells me I did a good job for my first day. I have a pocket full of Tootsie Rolls from Ms. Graves and a silver dollar from Mr. Peterson. I want to ask Dottie if it's okay to take tips, but if she says no, I'll have to give back that silver dollar, and I really don't want to. I'll ask Dottie tomorrow, once my silver dollar is safely tucked away under my mattress in the closet.

On my third day of work, I meet Mr. Valley. He has dark black and gray hair that pokes out of his ears and his nose along with his head. All of his features seem large to me. His earlobes hang like grapes; his nose threatens to overtake his face, and even his thick glasses magnify his eyes like saucers. I like him immediately, because he is such fun to look at.

Mr. Valley used to be a librarian when he was a younger man, over in East Bailey. He tells me his first wife was a bold, brassy woman who used to come in to the little red schoolhouse that had been converted into a library with her young son in tow. She claimed her husband had been a Navy man and died at sea, but Mr. Valley found out later that that wasn't exactly the case, and that the boy's father had never gotten around to marrying her at all before disappearing. She came in once a week and barked orders at Mr. Valley to find her something suitable for her son to read, books that would teach him about morals and values and the grace of God. Mr. Valley adored her immediately.

He asked her out to dinner one day while lending her a copy of *Oliver Twist,* and proposed to her the week he'd set aside *The Yearling* for her son's enjoyment. She was bossy and tempestuous, and Mr. Valley clearly still worshipped the ground she walked on, talking to me in his bright, buttery room at Sunny Brook.

The first Mrs. Valley had died of a particularly aggressive form of lung cancer when Mr. Valley was forty-five. Her son was nearly grown when this happened and went off to join the Navy like his absent father, leaving Mr. Valley alone in his grief. He turned to the church for solace.

Mr. Valley spent all of his spare time at Saint Matthew's, helping tend to the rectory garden and keeping the pews polished and the bibles neat and in order. He spent ten years there, sweeping the floor and shining the candleholders. Eventually he came out of his cloud of grief, and he began to notice the straight-backed, honey-blond woman who came to services faithfully every Sunday. He prayed to the Lord for guidance. The next Sunday, after services, the woman came up to him at coffee hour and told him she'd noticed the beautiful job he did with the church gardens and wondered what he would recommend for voles. Mr. Valley was smitten.

He helped the honey blonde, whose name was Eliza, with her vole problem, and her Japanese beetle infestation, and the aphids that threatened to destroy her vegetable patch. Eliza was a kind and gentle woman and had found herself shamefully divorced after her husband of thirty years finally revealed to her that after she'd borne him six children and raised them to adulthood, he no longer loved her. He added that he planned to marry his secretary, whom he'd been carrying on with for ten years. Eliza was stunned and a little lost. She'd left her father's house to marry her husband when she was sixteen and had never been on her own in the years since then. She'd turned to the only constant she still had left—her religion. It was an attitude Mr. Valley could appreciate in a woman.

He spent every Sunday afternoon helping her with her garden, and every Friday night, he took her out to dinner at the Green Leaf Cafe. He proposed to her while they were weeding her daffodil bed together, and at the age of 60, Mr. Valley found himself a married man yet again.

Eliza and Mr. Valley spent the next few years traveling, visiting her children who were spread out across New England. They bought a little house together and planted a lush flowerbed. They stopped at tag sales on Saturdays and attended services on Sunday, holding hands in the pew like blushing newlyweds as they listened to the sermon. It's clear as Mr. Valley tells me about his second wife that he was crazy about her, and I smile as I listen, leaning on the push broom I'm supposed to be using to sweep up his room.

Eliza started having problems with her memory about six years after she and Mr. Valley were married. Her speech was starting to sound a little funny, too, and she was worried that she might have had a small stroke. She went to the doctor and found out it was much, much worse: She had a cancerous tumor in her brain. Eliza was diagnosed in August and dead by November.

"So you see, Curtis," Mr. Valley tells me, "I was a lucky man. I had two great loves in my life. They were both taken from me too soon, but what kind of man would I be if I'd never known them at all? I've been blessed, very blessed," he adds. "Now I would like the Lord to take me home. Whenever you're ready, Lord!" he shouts up at the ceiling, but for now, his prayers remain unanswered.

What I really like about Mr. Valley is that he remembers things. I told him one time about how Nana used to bring home the expired Hostess products, and now, every Monday afternoon, Mr. Valley has a fresh package of Sno-balls waiting for me. Who is supplying him, I don't know, but I suspect Dottie might be his Hostess connection. "I know you like your sweets, Curtis," he says with a wink, and I peel off the cellophane and share a coconut-covered cake with him. And listen.

Mr. Valley is thrilled to discover my love for all things horror and has made a game of hiding classic novels throughout his room for me to find. I found Mary Shelley's *Frankenstein* under his bed one afternoon after he asked me to flip the mattress, and a couple of weeks later, a worn copy of *Dracula* tucked in behind the toilet that he suggested needed scrubbing.

Mr. Valley is my favorite resident at Sunny Brook. I know his second wife's daughter comes to visit every weekend with her two girls, but I never see them. That makes it easier for me to pretend that he's *my* grandpa.

15.

Penny Paradise works in the kitchen at Sunny Brook. I watch her smoke her cigarettes in the back parking lot when I leave work at night. She's got a round face, huge eyes, dimples in her cheeks, and short, spiky, blonde hair dyed pink at the tips. She's thin with a sharp nose, and looks like a baby bird learning to fly, all wings and fuzz. I've seen her at school before, and sometimes she's in the hall with the dopers, and other times she's in study hall with the brains. I can't pin down which crowd she hangs out with, but at least she has a crowd. My crowd is just Albert and me.

"Hey," she calls out to me one day as I'm shuffling across the parking lot, head down, hands in my pockets. Is she talking to me? I lift my head up slightly, and she waves me over, a white cigarette propped between her smooth pink fingernails. I hesitate, then make my way to her. Maybe she's going to try and get me to start smoking. Mom's always warning me that it starts with peer pressure.

"You and Mr. Valley seem pretty close," she says, and I nod. "Are you trying to get in his will or something?"

It's a terrible thing to say, and my cheeks go hot with anger. "Screw you, you nasty gash!" I spit out at her. It's the worst insult I can think of, and it's not even my own—I heard Bobby Foley taunting Pinky with this slur just last week. But unlike Pinky, Penny doesn't burst in to tears. She laughs and elbows me in the side like we've been friends forever.

"You're all right, Curtis Price," she smiles. "I'm Penny, by the way."

"Penny Paradise. I know. Who you are, I mean," I mumble. I'm still mad that she would even insinuate I want anything more from Mr. Valley than his friendship and the occasional Sno-ball.

"We're in the same homeroom," she continues. "Paradise, Price. Honestly, what are our parents thinking? I think it should be a law that parents should have to change their last names if it's going to brand their kids as dorks for life." She drops her cigarette on the concrete and puts it out with one neat twist of her heel.

Now she's talking about a topic I have spent many hours contemplating. "No kidding! Price is just so ordinary. And stupid," I add, waiting for her to agree.

"Please! You have it easy," she says, shaking her head. "Try being a girl with a name like Paradise. 'Hey baby, I'd sure love a night in paradise,'" she mimics, and I grin.

"At least your last name doesn't rhyme with *lice*," I say eagerly. "Bobby Foley spent all of seventh grade calling me Cursive Lice."

"Bobby Foley is a dickweed," Penny says decisively. "Cursive Lice doesn't even make sense."

I'm smiling so widely that my cheeks ache. Penny Paradise is all right.

We don't hardly see Dad anymore. He got remarried and moved to Pennsylvania. Mom says good riddance; he never paid child support on time anyway. His new wife, Heidi, is pretty and tall and a lawyer, information we gather from the picture and card she sends to me and Sally introducing herself and saying she hopes to meet us soon. What she's doing with Dad, Mom doesn't know, but he's her headache now. I'm a little sad and a little mad. It's not like we saw Dad all that much to begin with, and it was Mom who initially had to explain to me what wet dreams and hard-ons were. I kind of blame him for that. It really should have come from him, and now, whenever I'm popping wood in English class staring at Marcy Middleton, it's my mother's voice I hear in my head whispering *it's perfectly natural, Curtis; all pubescent boys go through this.* Which I guess isn't so bad after all, because there's nothing that makes me lose a hard-on faster than my mother's voice.

It's Heidi, not Dad, who sends me a check for $100 on my sixteenth birthday. This makes me instantly like her. Maybe it wouldn't be so bad to meet her someday.

I fail the driver's test twice. The first time, I flub the written exam; Penny helps me study before my second attempt, but then in the driving portion, I turn right on red which I think is allowed but turns out it isn't. The third time's the charm, and, of course, when the lady takes the picture for my license, I'm not ready and it looks like I'm about to sneeze in the picture on my ID. I'm not going to lie, though: it's still cool to be able to legally drive. Now I just need wheels.

Penny thinks I should get a truck, but I kind of want a car, like a Mustang or a Chevelle. "Don't be such a *guy*, Curtis," Penny grumbles, puffing away on one of our breaks. "Besides, a truck will be a lot more practical with the snow we get around here come winter."

Practical? Who wants practical? I just want to be able to impress Marcy Middleton.

With the money I've saved up from working at Sunny Brook, plus the fifty dollars Mr. Valley insisted on giving me "to help with your hot rod fund," I think I finally have enough money for a used car. It'll drain my EMT school fund, but I can start building that up again later. Finding a sweet ride is more important. I'm trying to keep an open mind. I'll settle for a GTO if I have to.

Penny comes with Mom and me to the car lot. Sally refuses to come with us. She dumped Derek Lombardo after he gave both her and Carla Devas crabs, but not before he found her a really good deal on a used heap. So she's got her own car now and certainly doesn't want me to drive her Granada, so she's supportive of my efforts to gain vehicular independence. But Sally thinks Penny is a freak, so she opts to spend the afternoon on the couch with her latest boyfriend, Steve, while we go car shopping.

We need Penny there because Mom and I don't know anything about cars and even less about haggling. Mom had suggested that we ask Mr. Jervis to join us, but I immediately shot that idea down, telling her that any jerkwad that drives a beat up, hideous Scout II clearly doesn't know the first thing about decent motor vehicles. Penny's father, on the other hand, is kind of a handyman, and can fix anything, including cars. He's nice enough to agree to come with us, since Penny has made it clear that she and I are just friends, and I am no threat to his daughter's virginity. Mr. Paradise is about seven feet tall, and skinny, with a wild mop of wavy dark hair. My heart flip-flops when I spot a white Dodge Charger, but Mr. Paradise shakes his head. "The mileage is terrible on these, and your insurance will be through the roof," he says. I don't care. I'll get a second job if I have to, but he tries again. "Look at this thing, Curtis. The floor's all but rusted out and the lining on the roof is shredded. Nothing about this screams 'I'm cool.' It screams 'I'm poor, and stupid to boot.'" This gives me pause. I can't really envision Marcy Middleton wanting to ride in a car with a body so rusted that it looks like it's been autopsied.

Eventually, Mr. Paradise finds a black Chevy truck with only 60,000 miles on it and a yellow lightning bolt detailed on the side. He's impressed that someone took care of the engine as well as they did, and Penny's happy that I'm getting a truck, just like she wanted. I won't admit it, but I want it for the lightning bolt on the side. You can just tell that whoever owned it before me got laid a *lot*.

It's a little over what I've saved, but Mom says she'll loan me the final $200 if it means she won't have to worry about me killing myself drag racing in a muscle car. I think I'll be able to drive it right off the lot, but it has to be registered and insured which takes time. Mr. Paradise takes us all out to Good Time Charlie's to celebrate, and Penny squeezes my hand under the table and winks at me during dinner. All in all, it's a good day.

16.

Mom drops a bombshell on Sally and me later that week. She and Mr. Jervis are now officially boyfriend and girlfriend. We should start calling him George, she announces, like this is the biggest thing she's been worried about. How about how he's a huge asshole? Mr. Jervis— my mistake, *George*—has eased up on the gold chains some, now wearing only two or three necklaces instead of the pound of plated tin he used to wear around his neck, but now he's taken to wearing his thinning hair in a ridiculous comb-over. When he's outside and the wind comes up, a long wisp of his black hair inevitably gets caught up and flaps in the breeze, causing his bright white scalp to flash underneath.

George and Mom go out to the Emerald a lot, staying so late that I'm often tucked into my closet, just drifting off to sleep when they come stumbling in, sometimes laughing, sometimes yelling. Tonight, when Mom tries to shush him because he's talking real loud, he tells her to shut her goddamn trap, he can wake up her kids if he wants to. Hasn't he been paying for the roof over our heads for a while now?

What the hell does that mean? I think, but then I remember one time Mom said that if it hadn't been for good neighbors, she never would've paid off that hospital bill from when I broke my arm.

Now that I think about it, she's been dropping in on Mr. Jervis— George—for some time now. Every time Mom started complaining about some unforeseen bill or surprise expense, her visits to George's side of the duplex increased. How long had she been borrowing money from that dickhead? Is he holding that over her now, like she's obligated to go out with him or something in return?

I resolve to talk to her about this—if we're that hard up for money, I'll contribute my paycheck each week, minus my truck expenses, like gas, of course.

I don't like George much, which is fine—I don't think he cares much for Sally and me, either.

Not that he hasn't tried to force niceties on us. George is a security guard at the Pinkham Ball Park, and he's always bragging about how he can get free tickets to any of the Swing Cats games. They're a minor team, and they don't win very often, but Mom insists that we should go to a game, since George is so generous to offer. We go once—me, Penny, Albert, Sally, Steve, and Mom. The popcorn is stale, the Swing Cats lose, and the first 1,000 people to come to the game get a free coloring book. I'm sixteen years old. What do I need a coloring book for? Penny spends the game filling hers in, giving the baseball players fuchsia hair and blue and green striped jerseys, which I will admit is the most entertaining part of the game. George preens with what I'm sure he is picturing as his ready-made family, introducing us to everyone at the ball field. Albert spends twenty minutes talking to the guy who wears the mascot jersey, trying to find out how one breaks in to the furry costume business.

George is loud and cocky, and he thinks he's better than all of us. He's also not very nice. There was a stray cat that was coming around to the back door occasionally, and Sally started feeding it, but then it started meowing at all hours, so George went out with his pellet gun one night and the cat was never seen again. I've heard him tell Mom a few times how nice it would be for us to move out of The Meadows and in to a real home. He thinks it's disgusting that I sleep in the closet. Sometimes I sleep on the couch, but it's a pain in the ass if Mom has to get up for an early inventory shift, because I inevitably wake up when she comes down at 3 a.m. Plus, Sally and I have our system down pat, and we haven't walked in on each other half-dressed in years. We give each other our private time, and at night, she and I stay up for about an hour after we've told Mom we're going to bed, talking about our day, who we like, what's going on at school.

Sally thinks that Steve is going to ask her to move in with him, and the way things are going with Mom and George, she just might leave, because she thinks he's an asshole too. She asks me if it makes her a bad person if she tries to get pregnant without telling Steve. I tell her it does. She thinks that if she's pregnant, Steve will marry her, and it will get her out of The Meadows permanently.

"Look at us, Curtis," she gripes, waving her hand around our room, which still has the same orange flowered wallpaper that it's had since we were kids. "I sure would like to live somewhere where people don't know how broke you are as soon as you tell them your address."

I want to tell her that if she gets pregnant at eighteen by a nineteen-year-old who flips burgers for a living, she's not going to get any richer. But I know what she means. I'm about tired of being a Meadows kid, too.

The worst times are late at night, when we hear Mom and George going at it in her bedroom. George is a grunter, and with every shove, he lets out a low *rruh!* sound. It's disgusting. I can't jerk off, because every time I try, I hear George's growling in my head. Poor Marcy Middleton hasn't starred in a fantasy in my head for weeks.

17.

Mr. Valley left me a copy of the new *Deadman* comic book under his mattress this afternoon. I still don't know who his supplier is, but he is the coolest old man I know. I thank him profusely, and he motions for me to sit down with him for a minute. "Curtis, I'm worried about you," he starts. "Do you have a girlfriend?"

I'm a little embarrassed that Mr. Valley has been spending his time wondering about my love life, but then again, he doesn't have much to occupy his days, so I guess a little speculation about the great conquests of Curtis Price is not unreasonable. "Nope," I admit.

"Well, why not? You're a good-looking young man. You've got broad shoulders and you're a hard worker. Any of those girls at school would be thrilled to have you ask them out for a soda."

Mr. Valley, nice as he is, has no idea what it's like to be in high school. I'm pretty sure *any* of the girls I know would shrivel up and die on the spot if I were to ask them out. And for a *soda*? Sometimes I forget how old Mr. Valley really is.

"Really, Mr. Valley, there's nobody."

"Really? Not one gal you've got your eye on?" he asks slyly, winking. I think about Marcy and crack a small smile before I can help myself. "Ah," Mr. Valley chuckles, patting my knee. "Who is she?"

I tell him about Marcy, with her soft auburn curls and bright green eyes. She still says hello to me in the hallways and even asked me a question about Ovid's *Metamorphoses* one day, even though we're not in the same English class anymore. It's like she has no idea how far out of my league she really is. Mr. Valley listens intently while I describe her and then shuffles to his dresser to rummage through the drawers. "You should tell her how much you like her," he advises solemnly, then turns back to me. "And give her this."

It's a thin, fragile bookmark with tiny gold scallops around the edges. There's a pressed rose in the middle of it. It's the most beautiful, delicate bookmark I've ever seen, and I hold my breath for a minute. It must be worth some real money. I can't take that from Mr. Valley, no matter how noble his intentions are. I tell Mr. Valley exactly that.

"Nonsense," Mr. Valley says, waving off my protests. "I gave it to my first wife when we were courting. It's what made her fall in love with me," he chuckles.

"Don't you want to save it for your stepdaughter?" I ask. After all, they're very close.

"I'm already leaving her everything else I own. She's a good girl, but what is she going to do with a bookmark that once belonged to her doddering stepfather's first wife? It's not like it was her mother's," he explains, and presses the bookmark in my hand. "I *want* you to have it. Every young man should have a romantic heirloom that he can impart on a girl to show her how crazy he is about her. *Take* it," he says again, voice raised, when I try to give it back.

I immediately carry it out cautiously to my truck to put it somewhere safe before I ruin it. I fold a paper towel around it and tuck it in to the glove compartment for safekeeping. I start to imagine a circumstance in which I can give it to Marcy. Now that we're juniors, I suppose I could stop her in the hall and ask her if she has a date to the prom.

Reality hits. What am I thinking? I can't ask her to prom. After all, I'm a guy from The Meadows. And she's *Marcy Middleton*. Star of the girls' soccer team and class treasurer. I'm sure she wouldn't even know who Wolverine was if he swooped into the hallway and stabbed Bobby Foley in the throat right in front of her—a frequent daydream of mine. I can't imagine any sort of circumstance in which I'd be able to look deep in to her eyes and press that delicate bookmark into her soft hands before leaning in for a kiss.

I know Mr. Valley's intentions are good. But I don't think I'll ever tell Marcy that I'm crazy about her.

Penny is waiting for me at the end of my shift. She's dressed all in black, smoking a cigarette and smiling like the Cheshire Cat.

"Let's go for a ride, Curtis," she says, tossing her butt and crushing it with her boot heel. I shrug and climb in to the truck.

"Where're we heading?" I ask as she slides in, immediately fiddling with the knob on the radio. "Wish You Were Here" by Pink Floyd fills the cab.

"The cemetery," Penny smiles, and I shift into gear.

I've never minded cemeteries. I find them calming, and I like to read the tombstones and try to imagine what the person's life was like who is buried there. What their death was like. Penny walks aimlessly through the rows, occasionally pointing out a short life and musing if it was cholera or just hard living that put them in the ground so young. She slows up so I can catch up with her and surprises me by taking my hand loosely, like it's the most natural thing in the world. My palms start to sweat.

"Curtis," she asks, peering up at me from under her bangs, "why is it that you've never made a move on me?"

"Uh," I stammer. Holy crap. How do I answer this? "Um … I guess … I guess I never thought you wanted me to. I didn't want you to—to get mad at me. I mean, I'm so … you're so …"

"Shut up, Curtis," she murmurs and gives me a kiss. My head explodes.

Penny and I make out for what seems like hours in the cemetery. She even lets me go under her shirt, and her tits feel so wonderful, I'm sure I'm going to burst. I can't believe I ever gave Marcy Middleton a second look. This is a *woman*, I think, stupidly. A woman right here and I've got a hand full of tit and a mouth full of tongue and *I love you. I love you, Penny Paradise.*

18.

I can't stop grinning as I drive Penny home. She's got her hand on my leg, and I'm so hard it's painful. Penny pretends not to notice, humming a song that I don't recognize at first. I realize it's "Rio" by Duran Duran, and I try not to laugh. I remember being so worried that I was gay after I'd had a wet dream about Nick Rhodes. If the tent in my jeans is any indication, I had nothing to worry about. A whole new world has opened up to me. A date for the movies, someone to take to the prom … people will refer to us as a couple. I am one half of a couple now. I think.

I stop the truck outside of her dad's house. "Um, Penny?" I feel stupid, but I have to know, before my hopes get so high they soar off the planet. "Are we a couple now?"

She laughs, a deep, rolling sound, like rain on the roof. "Oh, Curtis, we always were. You just didn't realize it right away." We have another minute of heavy kissing until she pulls away. "Don't get too carried away here," she whispers. "My father'll come out in the driveway with a shotgun." She gives me one last light peck on the lips and opens the door. "See you tomorrow, babe," she says and disappears inside her house.

My head is so high in the clouds that I don't even realize I'm driving home until I pull in. I'm too pumped up to go inside yet; I want to walk around the neighborhood, look at the stars, and think about everything that just happened with Penny, moment by moment. I stroll toward the ball field. I feel like skipping, but before I dare to give it a try, Bobby Foley steps out from the shadows near home base.

"Hey, douchebag," he says. "I got a bone to pick with you." And he punches the smile right off of my face.

I'm not sure what's going on, but I crouch and cover my head. I don't know why Bobby is so mad at me. I wonder wildly for a moment if he has a crush on Penny, if he could possibly know about tonight at the cemetery. He offers me a reason as he's kicking me in the ribs.

"I see the way you stare at Marcy. She's not for you, butt wipe. You'll never—" a punch to the head—"get a girl—" he kicks my stomach—"like Marcy. Pussy!" His fists continue to rain down on me, and the pain is unbelievable. I start to retch, and Bobby gives me one last kick to the gut before he strolls away. I throw up a stream of bloody vomit, and then I start to cry. I didn't even get a chance to tell Bobby I don't care about Marcy Middleton anymore. I have Penny. Or had her. She won't want to be with a guy who gets jumped for no reason and doesn't even defend himself. I stay on the ground, curled up in a ball, and cry hard, like a child who has lost a dog. I had a girl for about two hours. Now that rotten bastard Bobby Foley has taken her away from me.

Eventually I manage to pick myself up, slowly. My breathing is raspy, and I think a rib might be broken. I limp home and open the door quietly, trying to sneak upstairs without Mom and George hearing me. I can hear them both at the kitchen table, and I hold my breath as I start up the stairs. Why couldn't tonight be one of the nights they spend at the bar? No such luck. Mom is striding through the living room, ready to yell at me for coming in so late, but she gasps when she sees me.

"Oh, my God, Curtis! What happened to you? Were you in an accident?" She starts fussing over me and checking me for broken bones, and I can see George standing in the doorway of the kitchen, with his stupid comb-over. His cold eyes say one word, over and over: *pussy.*

Mom insists on keeping me out of school the next day, and she calls out of work to take me to the doctor's. I have a broken rib and a concussion, and by now I have a black eye and my cheek's so swollen, he's sure I broke a tooth. Then it's off to the dentist, and yes, I have a molar cracked down to the root. He pulls it and puts in a temporary crown, and I'm sent home for the next two days with my pain pills and orders to stay in bed. Mom keeps asking who did this to me, how did it happen, but I just tell her it was too dark to see. I can't have her going over to Bobby's father to tell him what his son has done. That would be too humiliating to bear.

George bitches and moans about how much my little fight is going to cost the family, as if he were a part of it. Between Mom's lost day of wages, plus the doctor's bill and the dentist, I have cost him a sweet penny. Mom tells him to hush up, we'll figure something out, but I just lay on the couch and groan. Mom thinks it's because I'm in pain, but mostly it's because I'm trying to drown out the sound of George bitching.

I'm heartsick over Penny, who I'm sure has heard what happened through the rumor mill at school. If not, I'm sure she'll quiz Dottie, since Mom called her to tell her I wouldn't be in to work for a couple of days. I'm positive she won't want to be seen with a loser like me. I didn't even get a punch in. Here I am, with broken teeth and ribs, and Bobby Foley doesn't even have a scratch on him. It's a good thing I'm doped up on pain medication; otherwise, the burning hate I feel for him right now would be unbearable.

Penny comes over after her shift at Sunny Brook with a tray of apple crisp from the cafeteria.

"Dottie sent it," she says, and then her forced smile cracks and tears stream down her face. "Oh, Curtis, why would he do this to you? What's *wrong* with him?" My eyes water a little, but I swipe my tears away before they can fall, because that would make it even worse. Penny doesn't seem to care. She sits on the edge of the couch and kisses my face all over, my bruises, my swollen cheek. She gently presses her lips against both of my eyelids. "You'll get him," she murmurs, and I look at her. "I know you'll get him, Curtis," she smiles. "Accidents happen. Tires get slashed, windshields shatter … you have plenty of time to get him back, Curtis. Don't worry about it now." She lays her head against my chest. I don't know how Penny got the impression that I'm some sort of vengeful superhero who rights wrongs, like Batman, but I like it. The cape she imagines me in feels good, and I wrap my arms around her, feeling better already.

19.

When I go back to school, my eye is still black, and I'm still walking a little gingerly. I don't say hi to Marcy in the hall anymore, because I don't want to give Bobby an excuse to start Round Two. She seems confused that I don't return her greeting in the corridor, but after a few days, she stops trying to get me to respond. I keep my eyes down on the ground and my bangs over my eyes. The only time I look up is during fifth period, when Penny and I have study hall together. Our time together flies by as we pass notes back and forth, stare at each other and lick our lips suggestively. I spend every moment that I'm not at school with Penny, even if it's at work. Mr. Valley wonders why I'm so happy with a broken rib. I don't tell him what happened before the broken rib, how Penny made her move and now I have a girlfriend, but he can tell.

"How's your girl today, Curtis? You treating her right?" I assure him with a shy grin that yes, I'm treating her just fine, and we fall in to our easy routine. I ask him for ideas for Penny's birthday. He suggests a pretty red cashmere sweater.

I really need to start asking someone who was born after 1920 for girlfriend advice.

Sally isn't much help either. When I ask her for gift advice, she tells me everything I shouldn't give her: condoms, lingerie, an apron, a vibrator. She starts to go back on her own advice—"on second thought, a vibrator might be the perfect gift"—but clearly she's not putting much thought into it. Mom suggests a teddy bear, but Penny has never struck me as the stuffed animal type. Indeed, she tells me that once, when she was in third grade, she dissected her Winnie the Pooh just to see what was inside. I decide to wander the mall myself and see what strikes my fancy. I find about thirty totally cool things in Spencer's, but mostly for me. I debate buying a KISS ARMY bumper sticker, then put it back. I don't think Penny would appreciate it if I gave her a bumper sticker for my truck.

On Penny's birthday, I pick her up at her house and take her out to Good Time Charlie's. She squeals in delight at the charm bracelet I give her, even though right before I hand her the box, I think about what a dumb gift it is. Nobody in high school wears charm bracelets anymore, and the cheap heart charm that I picked out to go with it seems corny. I'm such an idiot. But she puts it right on her wrist and swears she'll never take it off, says she's always wanted a charm bracelet and was always so jealous of the other girls who had tons of bangles on their wrists. She's kind enough not to say this was her wish back in fifth grade, but I suspect it was. She puts her hand on my crotch under the table and gives me a squeeze, and I decide to believe that she really does love it. Before we go to the cemetery for a little alone time, I pull in to The Meadows, parking the truck behind the baseball field where nobody can see it.

"Where are we going?" Penny asks, and I give her a wink.

"We're going to go put water in Bobby Foley's gas tank," I say, and she claps her hands in delight. "Best birthday *ever*," she breathes, and we sneak off in to the night.

20.

I drive Penny to school every day and wait for her outside the gym after last period so we can ride over to Sunny Brook together. I'm sure Dottie has noticed us holding hands and taking breaks at the same time, but she hasn't given us a hard time about it yet. Life is just about as sweet as it can get, except for Albert.

I'm not sure what his problem is, but lately he's been quiet at lunch, barely looking at me as he reads the latest issue of the *New Mutants*. He hardly talks except to say "sure" or "nope" as I endlessly pepper him with questions and observations, trying to get him to talk. Albert can be a total prick at times, but he's still my best friend and outside of Penny, he's all I've got.

We're sitting at lunch, Albert working hard on a rather impressive Colossus in his notebook, me peeling the cheese skin off of the cafeteria pizza, leaving the saucy crust on the tray.

"I'm thinking about taking Penny to Palace Playland this weekend. What do you think? Think it would be too cold?" I ask, mouth full of cheese. Albert slams his hand on the table, leaving a sharp blue slash across Colossus's massive chest with his ballpoint pen.

"I don't give a shit, Curtis. Take her to Playland. Take her to Mars for all I care. I am so sick of hearing about you and Perfect Penny! You two make me want to gargle my own vomit!"

Albert picks up his notebook with one swipe, causing his pen to clatter to the floor. He storms off, leaving me seething. How dare he!—Who does he think *he*—asshole! My best friend is a total, unequivocal asshole! I pick up my tray and throw it out, careful to head toward the opposite door from the one that Albert stalked off through. I stomp down the hallway, ducking in to the bathroom.

The place is empty, reeking of urinal cubes and cigarette smoke. I lean against the cold tile wall, still fuming. Albert's jealous, that's all. Little shit is never going to get a girl as hot as Penny, and he can't stand to see anyone else happy since he's so miserable. I should've punched him for being a dick. I look at the smudged paper towel holder hanging from the same wall I've been leaning against. I let out my best war whoop and punch it as hard as I can. The holder bends slightly, a small dent in testament of my rage. I wince; my hand throbs; I slide into one of the stalls and lock the door before anyone can come in and see me crying.

I'm silent with Penny on the ride over to the nursing home. She finally asks me what I did to my hand, since my knuckles are still red and swollen, and I grunt.

"What is your problem, Curtis Price? I'm in no mood to deal with your PMS today," she says out of the corner of her mouth as she lights a Marlboro.

"Sorry," I admit, not wanting to fight with her, too, even though I hate it when she smokes in my truck. "Al was a dick today, and I'm pretty sure we're not friends anymore."

"What? What happened?"

I tell Penny the story at lunch and even mention how Albert ruined a perfectly good Colossus during his temper tantrum. Penny shakes her head, takes another drag.

"He's just worried about losing you," she declares, exhaling. "You're his best friend, and you two were doing perfectly fine until I came along and ruined it all. He's jealous. He used to have you all to himself and now you're spending all your time with me. Remember," she adds, "you're *his* only friend, too. You're talking about taking me to Playland and that used to be something you'd probably be doing with him."

I shrug, not wanting to admit that she's right and I'm a lousy friend. "Well, what the hell am I supposed to do? He's like kryptonite to girls. He's fat and sweats too much and his skin is awful—I can't tell you how hard it is to eat lunch with him, with all those whiteheads on his cheeks. He'll never get a date. And all in all, I'd rather cozy up in the roller coaster with you, not him. Besides, when he gets scared, he farts. He can't help it. As soon as he gets nervous or anxious, *pfft*, out it comes. It's embarrassing going to a haunted house or a scary movie with him."

Penny laughs, shaking her head. "Listen, I've got a cousin in East Bailey who might just be Albert's speed. Julie's shy and smart and she loves to read everything, including comic books and Atari cheat guides. Why don't we go out to dinner, just the four of us, next weekend? It couldn't hurt."

It could if she rejects him, I think, but I just smile. I know Penny's trying to help. She's never been in a closed room with Albert when he crop dusts one of his sulfur bombs.

Albert's sitting alone at lunch the next day, at a different table than the one we're usually at, but still deep in the unpopular section where all the losers are quarantined. I slide in next to him and hold up my hand when he glares at me.

"I'm sorry," I say. "I'm sorry we haven't been hanging out as much, and I'm sorry for being a dick. I promise we'll hang out together tomorrow after school, just you and me."

Albert blinks at me, and then slowly nods. The very corner of his mouth is quivering, and I hope he doesn't start bawling in the cafeteria, because that would be the worst thing, looking like a baby in a room full of bullies. He takes a deep breath and waits it out for the moment to pass. "I'll think about it. Not sure I want to be hanging out with a loser like you."

21.

I broach the subject of Julie with Albert the next afternoon as we're in his room, taking a break from playing Pac Man to eat ice cream sandwiches. He's hesitant at first, and I know he's thinking about the fresh new zit that has just appeared on his chin, right in the middle. It's huge and red and chock full of pus, just waiting to burst right beneath the surface of his skin. I guess in a way, he's lucky that he gets these huge sporadic whiteheads instead of the small red pimples that dot my cheeks down to my neck every time I shave. "What's she like?" he asks, and I've never met her so of course I don't know, but I lie anyway.

"She's great, and so smart, and totally in to Atari and X-Men. She hates Depeche Mode and thought *Ghostbusters* was the best movie ever made," I lie, mixing in some of Penny in there.

"No, dude. What's she *look* like?" And I realize I don't know. Penny's at work so I can't call her to ask. I promise to find out and get back to him before he gives his final answer. Penny and I have agreed to go to Bubba Jack's BBQ on our double date, because I know the smoky rib platter is a hard temptation for Albert to resist, even if Julie turns out to be a total freakazoid. I get a brief description of red hair and freckles from Penny, and by Monday, Albert has agreed. Like he's doing me a favor.

Al and I get ready at his house that night. I'm wearing a blue denim button-down shirt and black jeans, which I know Penny likes. "They cup your ass just right," she's cooed when I've worn them before, and I'm hoping tonight might be the night we go all the way. Albert changes four times, from a polo shirt to a T-shirt, back to the polo shirt again. I convince him to go with a black button-down shirt with a Huey Lewis & the News concert tee underneath. He wears dress pants, which won't button over his belly all the way, but he wears a belt to cover it up. We drive over to Penny's house in Albert's mom's Crown Victoria, the only car any of us own that will fit all four of us. Albert passes gas twice on the way over, and I roll down all the windows before we get there, assuring him all the way that there's nothing to be nervous about, which is a total lie. I'm nervous too. If I can get my best friend a girl, maybe he won't mind so much when I'm hanging out with mine. But my hopes aren't high: look what I have to work with, and even though he cleans up okay, he still stinks pretty bad when he's jittery. *Maybe Julie will have a cold and not be able to smell anything*, I pray.

We get there, and Penny is wearing a powder blue mini-dress, a big change from the hot pinks and bright purples she normally wears. She looks smokin' hot and softer, somehow, and I grin like a goofball when I see her. She introduces us to Julie, a slightly round, short girl with frizzy red curls, pale green eyes, and freckles across her nose. She reminds me a little bit of the Strawberry Shortcake doll Sally had when she was little. She giggles nervously as she and Al shake hands, then sneezes.

"Sorry—allergies," she explains quickly, blowing her nose, and I say a silent prayer of thanks. Then we're off.

We make it to Bubba Jack's without any problem, but I keep my window cracked just in case. I sit in front with Al while Penny and Julie whisper occasionally in back. I ask Julie about school, and she's a sophomore at East Bailey. She's in French Club and works part-time at the McDonald's in town. We sit down to barbecue, and Al glares at me because I slide in next to Penny before he can protest. He must be crazy if he thinks I'm going to spend the evening sitting next to him, particularly since one of Penny's specialties is keeping her hand in my lap throughout dinner. Julie orders the same thing as Al, a smoky rib platter with green beans and loaded potatoes. Over dinner rolls, I see Al is sweating, and I scowl at him, move my head slightly towards Julie. Al clears his throat.

"So, Julie, how long have you known Penny?" I want to slap my hand to my forehead because I know I told him, but Julie just giggles.

"All my life, silly. We're cousins, remember?" Albert flushes red, but Julie just smiles. "Maybe Penny didn't tell you. It's okay," she adds, seeing his flushed face. "It's not like you failed the Kobayashi Maru or something," she says. Albert's jaw drops.

"You watch *Star Trek*?" he asks dumbly. Julie nods, tucking her chin down shyly. They spend the rest of the dinner discussing tribbles and hortas, the Klingon neutral zone and Romulan protocol, waving pork ribs around as they debate their points. Penny squeezes my hand under the table, and I lean over and give her a quick kiss on the cheek. I have the best girlfriend in the world. *I love you, Penny Paradise.*

22.

I didn't get laid the night of Albert and Julie's first date, but now Al is a lot easier to get along with. He's been floating on air the past week, and I'm pretty sure Julie gave him his first kiss ever—tongue, even. He's in love.

I'm all for being in love, and it's fine when it's my best friend, or me, but not when it's my mother.

One night when I'm sitting at the kitchen table, George comes in and grabs me by the arm so hard it leaves bruises.

"You little fucking shit," he screams, so close to my face that I can feel his spit landing on my cheeks. "You're gonna clean my truck up right good!"

"What're you—"

"Don't give me that bullshit innocent routine, I know it was you," George snarls, his fist cocked back like he's going to belt me, and hard. I don't know whether to duck, punch him in the gut first, or run.

"George, what are you—*Mom*?" I start to yell. "Mom, you home? George's gone crazy!" I hate the high pitch of my own voice, but I can't stop it. The man is off his rocker. I haven't done anything to him, except avoid him.

"Come on, you little shit," he says, dragging me by the shirt collar. I'm a little taller than him, but he's built like a brick shithouse, and I can't pull away from his grip. He hauls me outside, where his Scout is sitting, covered in a nebulous goo with streaks of yellow running through it.

Oh, shit. Someone egged his truck.

I knew I shouldn't laugh, but the sight of at least two dozen eggs splattered across George's prized piece of shit Scout is too much to take in. The laugh starts as a wheeze that I try to stifle, then erupts out in a full guffaw before I can help myself. He moves his fist from my shirt collar up to the back of my neck and smacks me, hard. The sharp pain knocks the snigger right out of me.

"George, what's going on?" Mom says from behind us.

"I'll tell you what's going on," George roars, whirling in her direction. "Your punk-ass son egged my truck and made a fucking mess, and now he's gonna clean it up. Ain't that right, Curtis? Otherwise, I'll put my fist into his guts and rip them out and strangle him with his own entrails. Disrespectful little fuck!"

"George," I wheeze, "I didn't do it. Where would I get so many eggs?" I add stupidly. *The grocery store?* I think, and hope George won't realize how flimsy my logic is.

"Shirking responsibility too, you fucking pussy? Goddamn, if you're gonna do something like this, at least man up about it. What a fucking coward." George is still scorching with anger.

"George. I didn't—listen, you go around the neighborhood, swerving your wheels at anyone walking near the road like you're gonna hit 'em. This was bound to happen." I am amazed at my own calm logic.

"Fuck *you*! That's just a little game between me and the neighborhood kids. All in fun. If you weren't so sensitive, taking things like a fucking pansy …"

"George," Mom interrupts. "If Curtis says he didn't do it, he didn't do it. Maybe it was Bobby down the street. He's always been a troublemaker," she muses.

George looks at her, teeth grinding, and turns back to me.

"You're cleaning it up," he hisses.

"No, I'm not," I say, indignant. "I'm late for work. Clean up your own fucking mess." I stalk over to my own truck, get in, and drive off before anything else can be said.

It must have been Bobby, of that I'm sure. For the first time, I'm jealous of him. Bobby is a cretin, but at least he has the balls to fight back when someone is being an asshole.

I thought that incident would give Mom a little insight into what a dick George really is, but no such luck. Mom and George are getting married. The guy is a total reptile, but Mom doesn't seem to see that at all. They go out drinking together every night, and by the time they come home, it's no use talking to Mom at all about how George left the ice cream out on the counter and didn't clean it up after it melted everywhere, or how he leaves his dirty underwear on the bathroom floor, which is just disgusting. Mom doesn't seem to mind, though, and every time I kick his stained boxers out to the hallway, she just picks them up with a sigh and whistles down the stairs.

And he still hasn't gotten his temper under control. A month ago I came home early from work and found George replacing the door to Mom's bedroom. The old one was on its side, caved in where someone had put a fist through it. I wanted to talk to Mom about it, but he was so sweet to her that week it was sickening, bringing her flowers and making us all hamburgers for dinner, and I never got the chance. But I sure as shit don't trust him.

Sally is hardly ever home any more, and I guess Mom doesn't care about that, either. Sally's always out with Hardy, her latest boyfriend, smoking cigarettes and pot out behind the movie theater where she works now. Steve fell by the wayside when she realized he was more interested in her friend Kelly than in her. Poor Sally—I suggest to her that perhaps cruising the strip mall in East Bailey is not the best place to find boyfriends, but she disagrees.

"I'm not gonna date any of the losers around here, Curtis," she says. "I've known these guys since kindergarten. How am I supposed to look at someone like Matt Phillips in the eye when I can still remember when he peed his pants in the first grade?"

"They can't all be like that," I say.

"Brad Schoonover played with himself in fifth grade. Jeff Watts always had boogers running down his nose. Eric Vaslyn sucked his thumb until seventh grade. This town is full of un-dateable guys."

Sally graduated high school last year and since then has been selling popcorn and sodas at the Showcase, stuck here in Osprey Falls like everyone else she knows. Except for Dave Ewing, who joined the army and wound up eloping with a girl he met in Germany. Now he has to live there because his girl was arrested once for drunk driving and the government won't give her a green card to come back to the United States with him.

The day of Mom and George's wedding, I have to work in the morning for a couple of hours. I'm looking forward to visiting Mr. Valley, telling him how Penny's going to be my date this afternoon at the horror show that will be Mom's nuptials. I enter his room, hiding a copy of Mark Twain's *Short Stories* behind my back that I found at the library book sale and thought he might like.

Mr. Valley's bed is empty, and then I realize Dottie is right behind me.

"Oh, Curtis. I wanted to tell you before you got to his room. Mr. Valley passed away last night. He went peacefully, in his sleep. I'm so sorry, Curtis. I know how you two got on so well."

I sit on the edge of Mr. Valley's bed, stunned. I can still smell his Old Spice, catching in the corners of the room. My eyes fill and I wipe them away, quickly, but not before Dottie sees. She sits down next to me and gives me a smothering hug, which makes me feel even worse.

"I'm okay, Dottie. I'm okay," I mutter, standing up quickly, breaking her hold. I look around the room for a minute, lay down the Twain book on the dresser, and slump out. I find Penny outside and ask for a cigarette. Seems like a good time to start, but I inhale, cough, and hand it back to her. She doesn't know what's happened, and I tell her. She starts to cry, more than enough for the both of us, and now I'm hugging her, trying to comfort *her*. We stand like that for a minute, her shoulders shaking against my chest. She pulls back, looks in to my eyes with her reddened ones, and apologizes.

"Oh, Curtis. What're you going to do now?"

I shrug. Not much to do, except get ready for Mom's wedding. This is promising to be one of the worst days of my life.

Mom is wearing a beige silk pantsuit for her big day, which makes her look airy, like a butterfly. George is wearing a suit that's too small for him, and he can't even button the jacket. He looks red and sweaty next to Mom, whose eyes are glassy, making me think she's had a few pops before reciting her vows. The ceremony is being held in our tiny backyard, and Mom borrowed a bunch of metal folding chairs from the community center for the twenty or so people that are invited. I have to stand at the altar next to George, who was at least smart enough to not make me his best man, seeing as how I can't stand him. His pal Budweiser Rob from the bar is best man, and I'm standing next to him, getting a whiff of how he earned his nickname. I watch Mom, who looks woozy, and Sally, standing next to Mom, stuffed tight in a pink mini dress, her bangs teased up high like some sort of sad rocker chick. I look at Penny, who is shifting uncomfortably in her hard, metal seat. She has dyed her hair white-blonde for the wedding, and she reminds me of the girl from the Romantics. Gorgeous. As always.

We make it through the vows, and I remember the rings, so I've done my part. Mom asks Penny to take a picture of her with her kids on her wedding day, and Penny obliges. I smile for the photo, mostly because George isn't in the picture with us. I kiss Mom on the cheek and leave her to her friends, who are gathered around the keg that's by the tree, packed in a garbage can full of ice. George is barking out orders to anyone who will listen, telling Budweiser Rob to go get his pistol so he can shoot the squirrels that dare to run up the trees near the back lawn during the celebration.

Penny and I walk, hand-in-hand, down to the baseball field. It's dusk, and the night is cool, so I give Penny my suit jacket. We sit on the cold, steel bleachers and watch the sun set, my arm around her shoulders. I swallow hard and finally tell her what I've been thinking since the first night at the cemetery.

"I love you, Penny," I admit, my heart in my throat. *Please, whatever she says, don't let it be "thank you,"* I pray quickly. She smiles at me, kisses me once, softly, on the lips.

"Well, that's a good thing, because I love you too, Curtis Price."

We sneak in to the community center and lay my jacket down on the dirty floor, and Penny hands me a rubber. She unbuttons my pants, and I unzip her dress, and soon, we're naked and sweaty and fumbling. When we're done, which is quicker than I would have liked but still the most fantastic thing that's ever happened to me, Penny lights a cigarette.

"Goodbye, Mr. Valley," she whispers, and I echo her. *Goodbye, my friend. Thank you for telling me that wonderful things really do happen to ordinary guys like me. Goodbye.*

23.

Sally is pregnant. She told me today, and she wants to marry Hardy in the back yard, just like Mom and George's wedding. George goes apeshit, telling her over his dead body, and she's going to have an abortion whether she likes it or not, which is ridiculous. George isn't our father and isn't allowed to say one damn thing about it, according to Sally. She and Hardy will go live with our real father and Heidi out in Pennsylvania, she announces tearfully, which has to be a lot better than *this* shithole town. George asks her if she's called her real father yet, stand-up guy that he is, and she marches out of the room to call him, only to find that his number has been disconnected.

Hardy seems okay with being a dad at first. He works mowing lawns for his friend Sean, who has his own landscaping business, and Sally says he makes real good money in the summer. Mom invites Hardy over for dinner and asks him over a plate of spaghetti with meatballs where they intend to live.

"Here, I guess," Hardy shrugs, and Mom gently explains that that is not possible, what with me already sleeping in a closet. There's not enough room for one more person, let alone a new husband and a baby. They are going to have to live with Hardy's parents, or, ideally, find a place of their own. Has he gone in to town yet to look for apartments? There's one for rent right above the Emerald, as a matter of fact, if he doesn't mind the noise from the bar underneath. Plus, when there's a line for the bathroom, sometimes a drunk or two will duck in to the stairwell leading up to the apartment and piss on the steps. But for a newlywed couple with a new baby, you take what you can get, don't you? Hardy is looking paler and paler as Mom continues. Has Hardy thought about getting a full-time job? This baby's due in December, and Sally won't be able to work for a couple months after it comes. What will he be doing to support them?

Sally is tearfully optimistic, insisting that as long as she and Hardy love each other, they'll be fine. Hardy does not look like a man in love. He looks sick.

The next day, Hardy stops by the house, calling Sally outside. She's in a white spring dress and her hair is pulled back with a ribbon the color of butter, and she looks practically angelic, standing out there, leaning in towards him, smiling. The smile doesn't stay on her face long. Hardy clearly has bad news for her. They talk for a minute, Hardy gesturing wildly while she shakes her head, and as I sip my morning Pepsi, watching from the window, I unconsciously shake my head with her.

"Mom?" I try to call out as softly as possible, watching my sister grow redder and redder, knowing she's about to storm inside. "Mom?" I call out, a little louder. "I think Sally's going to need you. Mom!" I hear the door to her bedroom open up, just as Sally slams through the front door.

"Mooooommm! You've ruined my life!" Sally screeches, sobbing. Mom comes quickly down the stairs, holding her robe closed with one hand and holding her arm out to Sally with the other. She pulls her in, letting her whole body shake as she enfolds her in her own.

Hardy has broken up with Sally. He doesn't want to get married, doesn't want to settle down, isn't ready to give up Friday night pool games with the boys just yet. Sally tells Mom all this on the couch while I sit on the stairs, grateful George is at work and not here to tell her "I told you so." Sally holds out a fistful of crumpled bills. Hardy has given her a hundred dollars toward an abortion.

"'Take care of it,' he said," Sally wails. "He was telling me a week ago that the only thing he loved more in the world besides me was this baby! How could he do that?" Mom keeps her arm around Sally and rocks her, murmuring that it will be okay, it will all be okay: they'll get through this together.

Mom makes an appointment for Sally to go to Mom's gynecologist. They go on a Tuesday, and that night, Sally whispers to me as I lean back in my closet that the abortion is scheduled for Saturday. She's scared, she says. I tell her Mom will be with her, and it will all be fine. She says she's still hoping Hardy will show up and tell her he's sorry, that he made a mistake and he really does want her and the baby after all. I don't know. Hardy never struck me as much of a responsible family man.

Mom takes the day off special to bring Sally to her appointment. I work at the nursing home all day, but Penny isn't working today and without Mr. Valley there, I don't enjoy going in like I used to. I mop and dust and listen to Mrs. Fay talk about her dead husband Winston. I wonder if old Mrs. Fay ever had to worry about things like abortions. When I get home, Mom and George are eating a quiet dinner in the kitchen. I make myself a plate and sit down with them.

"Where's Sally?" I ask, pouring a glass of milk.

"Upstairs. She wants to be alone right now, Curtis, so maybe you can sleep down here on the couch tonight. How does that sound?" Mom leans over and ruffles my hair like I'm a little kid again. George just grunts, probably upset that me being on the couch will interfere with his plans to watch *Cops* all night. I shrug and nod. I'm nervous about seeing Sally. Will she be different? Will she be happier, now that this problem is over? Or will she be crying, still waiting for Hardy to show up?

I'm sleeping on the couch when I hear a noise in the kitchen that wakes me up. I rub my eyes and get up, shuffling in to the kitchen. Sally's there, standing by the sink, staring out the back window. She's nursing a glass of what appears to be orange juice, but Mom's bottle of vodka is uncapped on the counter next to her.

"Hey, should you be drinking that?" I ask stupidly.

Sally glances over at me, takes another swallow. "I guess if I'm old enough to kill my own baby, I'm old enough to have a drink or two, don't you think?" Her tone is sharp, and I shrink back. I was going to hug her, but hearing the edge in her voice, I abandon that plan. I sit at the table.

"You okay?" I ask, and she turns to glare at me.

"No, Curtis, I'm not okay. I don't know if I'll ever be okay again." A fat tear starts tracking its way down her cheek. "I tried to call Hardy tonight to let him know I'd done it. He wouldn't even come to the phone." She shakes her head. Her hair is flat against her head, like she's been in bed for a while. Sally takes another sip of her drink and lets out a harsh laugh. "I guess I should be happy. Nobody's going to be calling me the town slut now." She says it like she's joking, but I'm not sure.

"I won't tell anyone," I say, hoping this will make her feel better. "Not even Penny."

Sally snorts. "That's exactly who you *should* tell, fucktard," she says. "Wait until I run away and get out of this nowhere town, and then tell her. Tell her you can't trust any guy, not even you." She pours more vodka into her glass, then adds a splash of orange juice.

Now I'm pissed. I'm not anything like Hardy, who never even bothered to finish high school and got busted for stealing a car before he turned sixteen. I never do anything, for chrissake. I go to school and hang out with my one friend and go to work and read my comics and occasionally get beat up for no reason. Hardy has always been in trouble, and Sally should have known better than to tie up with a loser like him. I tell her this. Sally tells me to fuck off, then runs back upstairs, crying.

She started it.

24.

Penny's got mono, and I can't be around her for two weeks. I've been hanging around with Albert some, but now that he has a girlfriend, he's busy a lot more and doesn't have as much time for me. I guess this is payback for all the times I blew him off for Penny, so I can't really get mad at him. I spend a lot of time at the library, checking out the latest Stephen King and Jack Ketchum books. I have a harder time with Ketchum, since his descriptions are brutal and make me squirm. He actually grosses me out a lot. Not that I would ever admit this, and every time I see someone from school looking through the stacks, I make sure to prop my book up so they can see what a badass I am, reading *The Girl Next Door*. I don't know why I bother, though. Nobody ever looks my way. The lady behind the checkout desk always calls me Carl, even though it says Curtis right on the library card I hand her.

Sometimes after the library, I stop at Rexall to buy some Spree or Mentos candy. Then I flip through their rack of comic books until I get kicked out. The old man who runs the place is really short-tempered, but Stinky Pinky works there some afternoons, and she lets me stay as long as I want. She always smiles at me and gives me a soft "hi" when I come in, and I usually nod. She's still the pariah of Osprey Falls High, and as much of a loser I am, my reputation would be absolutely ruined if anyone saw me talking to her, even at the pharmacy. I already know how bad it is to be associated with her, and I don't need a repeat performance of that. At least most people don't even notice me, and there's something to be said for that. People like Bobby Foley actively seek Pinky out to make her life miserable. I heard last month that someone put a used maxi-pad in her locker, and just a couple of weeks ago, someone in her gym class cut a big hunk of her hair off in the shower. I do feel bad for her and won't be deliberately mean to her. But we can't be friends. I have to save myself.

To celebrate the end of Penny's quarantine, I take her for a picnic on the beach. It's a bit of a drive, and she's still real pale, but she insists she's up for it. I ask Mom to help me pack some food. Mom's just relieved that I didn't catch mono myself, which I guess reassures her somehow that I'm not having sex, and she's happy to help. Honestly, it's nothing short of a miracle that I didn't catch it, but I'm not going to tell Mom that. We make potato salad and fried chicken and chocolate chip cookies. Mom laughs at my attempts to peel the potatoes after they're done boiling, and I drop the first one on the floor just about as soon as I pick it up.

"That's freakin' hot!" I yell, and Mom is doubled over, clutching her stomach because she's laughing so hard.

"Sally, come in here and help your brother learn how to cook," she calls out, wiping tears from her eyes with a dishtowel. "He just figured out why that game is called Hot Potato." Sally says nothing, as usual. She's in the other room, listening to her Walkman. Mom shakes her head and turns back to the potatoes. "Peel them under cold running water, Curtis," she tells me, and I have them done in no time. It's nice to see Mom laughing and relaxed for once, and I try to deliberately screw up the cookies, just so I can spend a little more time with her when she's like this. I can't mess up too much, though, because as Mom eventually points out, I'm going to be late picking up Penny.

"Don't be out too long," Mr. Paradise tells me sternly as he shakes my hand. "She's still worn out from being sick." I promise to go easy on her and immediately curse myself for saying such a thing to her dad. I'm always terrified that he's going to find out Penny and I are doing it, and my nervousness about saying the wrong thing has me saying the wrong thing all the time. Penny smiles and pats my arm, and we leave before I can blurt out something horrible about condoms or my sister's abortion.

Ocean Beach is deserted this time of year, since it's still too cold to get in the water, though the air is warm. We find a spot next to a hunk of driftwood that shelters us a little bit from the wind, and I spread out the old blue blanket that I've been sleeping with in the closet for years. We settle down, and I pull out the potato salad bowl covered in plastic wrap and the fried chicken.

"I helped make this," I admit shyly, and Penny squeals. She stubs her half-smoked cigarette out in the sand and leans over to hug me.

"You cooked for me? I don't believe it!"

"It's true; ask my Mom," I say, and Penny kisses me quickly on the lips, then leans in for a longer kiss. Is she still contagious? I decide I don't care if she is.

"Well, if you cooked for me, you must really love me," Penny murmurs, and I nod.

"I missed you so much," I admit, and we lay back on the blanket, holding each other, chicken forgotten. "I don't know what I'd do without you."

Penny strokes my face, studying me.

"Well, good. Because I don't know what I'd do without you either."

We spend the afternoon fooling around and looking for starfish and picking up random shells. It might be the best afternoon of my life, and not just because I get laid. Twice.

When I get home later, I can't wait to find Mom and tell her what a great time Penny and I had, and thank her for helping me with the picnic. But Mom's not home, Sally's asleep, and I nod off on the couch waiting for Mom to show up. Mom and George finally come in around 2 a.m., the sound of their footsteps on the stairs waking me up.

"Mom?" I call out, and I hear her sigh. I rub my eyes and look up. Mom's cheek is swollen, and her left arm is in a sling. "What the fuck?" I say, then wince. I don't think I've ever sworn in front of my mother before. I offer a quick apology and look at George's blank face. He stares back, giving away nothing.

"Now don't get excited," Mom says, but her eyes look red and runny, like she's been crying. "I fell down the stairs. I had an armful of laundry and couldn't see where I was going, and I missed a step. Hit my cheek pretty good against the railing, too," she explains, offering a nervous laugh and gingerly touching her puffed cheek.

"Jesus, Mom, are you okay?" I ask. "Is it broken?"

"My wrist is sprained is all, and my shoulder's bruised. I'll be fine," she says, waving me off with her good arm. "Go back to sleep. Is your sister upstairs?" Normally I'd say something smart about not being my sister's keeper, but now is not the time, and it's not like Sally leaves the house much these days.

"I think so. Wake me up if you need anything tonight, okay, Mom?" I say.

"I can take care of her," George says, almost whining, and I look at him sharply. George is not known for his complacency. My eyes narrow. *What's going on here?*

Before I can ask, Mom kisses my forehead and tells me good night. George helps her up the stairs, almost cradling her, and I lie back down on the couch.

Just as I'm falling asleep, it occurs to me that the washer and dryer are upstairs, along with the bathroom and all of the bedrooms. The only laundry Mom brings downstairs is clean kitchen towels, and even then, it's a stack of three at most. How is that an armful?

25.

I'm still suspicious that George had something to do with Mom's injury. I hate this asshole and want him out of our lives. Now.

My plan, when it finally comes to me early one morning, is brilliant. If George loses his job, then he can't pay the bills, and Mom won't be dependent on him for money anymore, which can be the only reason, really, why she's keeping him around. With him gone, Mom and I can pay the bills, and Sally too, if she can get another job after losing the one at the theater for not showing up anymore after the abortion. I sneak downstairs early, before anyone else, and let the air out of his back passenger-side tire. A flat tire ought to make him late for work.

I forget about the tire during the school day until that night, when George grumbles about it at over dinner. "Tires are old," he mumbles, mouth full. "I've needed new ones for a while. Shoulda expected this," he says to no one in particular. Sally and I eat in silence, as quickly as possible, just to get away from the table.

About a week later, there's a message on the answering machine from George's boss saying he needs to come in early for his shift the next day. *Do I really want to do this?* I think. Then, *if he loses the job, he's out of our lives.* I hit the erase button and head over to Sunny Brook.

George is in an exceptionally nasty mood the next evening. "That fucking retard bastard has the *nerve*—? Nothing would ever get done at that shit show if it wasn't for me!" He's in the kitchen, shoving chairs and stomping in a circle hard enough to make the plates in the cabinets shake. I motion to Mom, who slips out of the kitchen and follows me outside.

"What's going on?" I whisper.

"Nothing. George's upset because he was written up at work for tardiness. I don't blame him—it's not like he could control a flat tire or a shift change that they never even told him about."

"Mom," I ask, softly. "Do we really need him? If he loses his job, I mean … well, between you, me, and Sally, our paychecks …" I trail off.

Mom glares at me. "Curtis, I really don't appreciate this. George is my husband, and I love him. I wish you'd make more of an effort to get along with him." She shakes her head at me slowly, like she's disappointed at me, and then goes back inside. "Let's go down to the Emerald for a bit," I hear her tell him.

Great. Because that'll *solve everything*, I think.

After they leave, I sneak into their bedroom, unscrew the back of George's alarm clock, pop a gear, shake it to make sure it's now broken, and screw it back shut. *Third tardy could be the charm*, I hope.

Three nights later, Mom and George insist we have dinner together at home, all four of us sitting at the kitchen table like a regular family. Mom makes baked pork chops with rice and green beans, and it smells pretty good as I scrape my chair against the vinyl floor, the cheap tiles yellow with age. Sally's next to me, hair unwashed, eyes downcast, slumped in her seat, the way she always looks lately. I pick up my fork to dig in but Mom stops me, announcing that she and George have big news. Great news, she insists.

"We're moving to Connecticut," she beams. "George got a great job offer, working security for the big stadium down there in Hartford. They even have their own hockey team. Doesn't that sound wonderful?"

I drop my fork. All my work sabotaging his job, and the bastard was looking for a new one all along?

"Are you fucking kidding me?" I blurt, and George leans over the table, slapping me soundly before I can dodge his meaty palm.

"Hey!" Mom shouts, but George turns toward her, hand still raised, and she cowers backward into herself, flinching.

"You don't use that kind of language in front of your mother," he says, frowning.

"No way," I say, slamming my palms down on the table, making my pork chop jump on its plate. "I'm not going."

"You don't get to make that decision," my mother says, her voice shaking, rising. "You're my son, and you live by my rules until you're old enough to vote and go to war. You're going." Mom's face is turning redder with every clipped word.

Sally remains silent, and I quickly realize I'm not going to get any help from her. I'm sure she doesn't care where she goes, as long as it's away from Hardy, away from this town, away from her humiliation and heartbreak. Tough shit. I continue ranting.

"It's not fair! You people've kicked me around my whole life! I'm finally in a good place, and you want to take it from me! I won't leave my job, and I won't leave Penny! You can't make me! I'm tired of being the kid in the closet that will just make do with whatever you throw at me. I'm not going!" But I can see, as George rolls up his sleeves and hot tears stream down my face, that I don't really have a choice at all. I'm moving to Connecticut.

George gets up, and, in one quick motion, has me out of my chair and up against the wall, his hand circling my throat.

"George!" Mom gasps. He ignores her; squeezes my neck, just a little.

"Listen to me, you snot-nosed brat. I don't know why you think you're entitled to have a say in this, but you don't. So shut up and start packing, and if I hear one word of complaint from you, I'll rip off your head and shit down your throat. Got it?" He's spitting as he yells, and for a moment, I think, *he could kill me right now if he wants to.*

As suddenly as it happened, it's over. George lets go and sits back down to tuck into his pork chops. "You can't *do* that," I sputter, furious, my chest hitching for air. "I'll—I'll call the cops. You can't drag me to Connecticut if you're in jail for assaulting me, you fucking criminal."

George looks up at me with black eyes, still chewing. "Call 'em," he says. "I think they'd be very interested to see our little living arrangement. By the way, genius, it's illegal, you and your sister sharing a room like you do. They'll pull you out of here so fast, it'll make your head spin. Probably put your mother in jail for neglect. So go ahead and call. See what happens."

Is he right? He might be. Shit.

Mom sits at the table, not eating, crying silently, her arm still snug in its sling. I storm out of the house, leaving my half-eaten dinner behind. I want to find Penny, but she's not home, and her father doesn't seem too keen on me stopping by after dusk when there's school tomorrow. I drive over to Al's instead, and he lets me in. I try to tell him about the move, but I start blubbering so hard that I can't get it out. He pours me some Pepsi and lets me cry, and when I finally get ahold of myself and can catch my breath, he hands me some Kleenex and tells me I have snot running down my face. Not once does he call me a pussy. How can I leave my best friend?

When I finally tell him the whole story, he gets pissed. Al's wearing a dorky Hulk Hogan tee that he bought the time his uncle took us to the wrestling show in Bangor, and in an act of solidarity, he tears it apart, just like the Hulkster. Well, almost like him—Al struggles a bit, but once he gets the rip started, he growls, showing his outrage. I finally crack a smile, and he sits down again.

"Can't you move in with your dad?" he asks, but I shake my head. I don't even know where he's living, and Mom complains all the time that he owes her thousands of dollars in child support. I guess I've never mentioned that to Al.

"I'll talk to my parents. You can move in here with me. George can't make you move right before senior year. That's bullshit." He throws his torn shirt to the carpet for emphasis.

I agree with everything he's saying, and we make a plan. He'll talk to his parents and I'll move in here. I can use the guest room that's right down the hall from him, and we'll drive to school together every day. I have to admit I'm excited about the idea of having my own room for the first time in my life. I'm a little too big to be living in a closet, and I don't want Mom to get arrested.

I drive home slowly, feeling good. I take care to sneak in to the house as quietly as possible, so Mom and George don't hear me. I don't feel like telling them tonight that I'm really, truly not going to

Connecticut with them. I hide my smile as I make my way through the dark to my bed, careful not to disturb Sally. She's curled up, facing away from me, and I can tell by her breathing she's still awake. If I wanted to, I could cajole her into staying up and talking this whole thing over with me, but I don't want to discuss it if she's not going to be happy for me. Sally can't even get excited about getting out of bed these days, so I slide my closet door shut and slip into a fitful sleep.

The next day at school, Albert won't look me in the eye. Uh-oh. At lunch, he tells me he waited up last night for his parents to get home and asked them. His father called me a juvenile delinquent who read too many comic books, and his mother said she didn't mind me so much, but she has her doubts about "that Paradise girl." She doesn't want to encourage any fooling around under her roof. If I would agree to break up with Penny, she'll consider letting me move in, but only after she discusses it with my mother.

My heart sinks. Out of the question.

I had no idea Albert's parents thought so little of me, especially since I hardly ever see them. I thought they'd be thrilled that their son had a friend, the only one he's ever had practically his whole life, but they don't seem to care. They just want Albert to stay out of their way. They might be disturbed once in a while if there were two boys in the house instead of one.

I have to work at the home that afternoon, and Penny's leaning against my truck, blowing smoke rings, when I get out of my final class for the day. She's wearing a turquoise dress that looks all gauzy and loose like curtains, but with her blue-streaked blonde hair, it just makes her eyes shine brighter. She gives me a quick kiss on the lips and slides in to the truck.

"Dad said you stopped by last night. What's going on?"

I can't tell her, not yet. I shake her question off and we drive over to Sunny Brook in silence. I've got my Guns 'N Roses cassette playing, and the opening bars of "Sweet Child o' Mine" start up right as we pull into the parking lot. I put the truck in park and turn to her, give her a kiss. I can't talk. I'll wait until after work.

I swab floors, wipe down surfaces, and dust TV screens mindlessly, wondering how I'm going to tell my girl I'm leaving her. I hate Mom for making me do this. I wonder briefly if there's any way to get George arrested, since he's the one making us move. Maybe I can call the cops one night when I know he's been drinking and get him thrown in jail for DWI. But if he suspects me at all, he'd just turn around and tell them about me and Sally sharing a room, and Mom would wind up in trouble. No good. I accidentally use Lysol instead of Pledge on Mrs. Orlomoski's dresser. She immediately starts coughing, which is difficult with her oxygen tube, and one of the nurse's aides comes running in, glaring at me. I skip break time with Penny.

When my shift is over, Penny is standing right outside the exit, arms crossed.

"What the fuck is your problem today?"

Looks like we're about to have our first fight. The anger bubbles up to my throat and all the bile that I want to spew toward Mom and George and Albert's parents comes out at Penny.

"What's my problem? You're my problem. Get off my back! If I want to talk about my problems, I'll talk. Stop being so goddamn needy!"

Penny blinks at me for a moment. Then she hauls back and slaps me so hard I feel my teeth shake.

"Screw you, Curtis Price. Fucking asshole. Stupid fucking fuck." She spins on her chunky heel and stalks off in the direction of her house, which is seven miles away. Let her walk. Nosy, nagging …

I can't let her walk. None of this is her fault. Plus, if I apologize, maybe there's still a chance of getting a hand job in her driveway tonight.

She's walking pretty fast, but I catch up with her easily with the truck. "Penny, come on. I'm sorry. Please get in the truck. I'm sorry."

She flips me the bird and keeps on walking.

"Come on Penny. I've just had a bad day. Please get in the truck."

Double birds this time.

"Damn it, Penny. I'm moving to Connecticut. Get in the fucking truck!"

She stops, turns to me. "What?"

"Please get in the truck. Come on."

She pulls her purse strap higher on her shoulder, hesitates for a moment, and climbs in. "What?" she says again, looking at me, her eyes wide.

I pull over in to the Dairy Queen parking lot and shut off the engine. "George got a job in Connecticut. He leaves next week to sign the contract on a house, and we're moving as soon as school ends. I'm moving."

She starts to cry, and I want to too, but I just hold her instead, kissing the top of her head. She says I can't move, she'll talk to her father and see if I can move in with them, but I don't have high hopes. Al's parents said no pretty quickly, and I'm not even sleeping with him.

Of course Penny's father is against the whole idea and even though she tells him he's the cruelest, meanest father in the world and she'll hate him forever, he still won't budge. I'm right back to square one. I'm moving to Connecticut.

26.

Even though I'm miserable, Mom seems carefree and excited about the move. George has gone ahead to Connecticut, and there's a lot less static in the air at home without him around. Mom even agrees to pay for half my tux rental for the junior prom, so I try not to sulk too much or push too many buttons in the week leading up to the big night.

Al's borrowed his mom's Crown Vic again, and he and I drive over to Penny's house to pick up her and Julie. Mom follows behind us in her car, because she wants to take pictures. When we arrive, all elbows and sweat and corsages, Mr. Paradise opens the door quickly. Mom says hello and goes upstairs to help Penny and Julie finish up their makeup.

"Hello, boys. The girls are just finishing up getting ready, so let's sit for a minute and chat, shall we?" He escorts us to the kitchen table and taps the backs of two chairs. "Here," he says, and we sit.

"I want you all to have a nice time tonight," he starts, lacing his fingers together, then stretching them in front of him, palms out. "And I want the girls home by midnight. Not a minute later, understand?" he says, pointing at me.

Hey, Al's the one driving, I want to say, but instead I mumble "yessir."

"I expect those girls to be just as sober when they come home as when they leave the house tonight. If they smell like alcohol, I'm coming to your house, and it won't be pleasant. If they smell like mouthwash, I'm coming to your house. If they smell like perfume, I'm coming to your house. And guess what happens if their hair or clothes look even the tiniest bit disheveled?"

"You're coming to my house?" I blurt. I'd been hoping for a little after-prom sex tonight, but now I'm not so sure it's a good idea.

"That's right, Curtis. You're a smart young man," he says. "Say, have I ever showed you my gun collection? Uh-oh—no time for that now. Looks like the girls are ready!" He smiles broadly and gets up from the table.

Al and I exchange an anxious glance and follow Mr. Paradise. "Dude, you didn't get any alcohol, did you?" I whisper.

"From who? My cool older buddies that I hang out with all the time?" he hisses back. I'd managed to swipe a half a bottle of Mom's vodka, but I don't think I'll be bringing that out later after all. We shut up as Mom comes downstairs and aims her camera up the staircase.

Penny is wearing a cherry-red strapless gown that hugs her boobs and hips before flaring out in a ruffle. Her bangs are dyed pink to match her lipstick. She is beautiful. I'm pretty sure my heart has stopped beating.

"You clean up nice," she murmurs as she hooks her arm in mine and poses for Mom. I grin like an idiot. I'm dating the most gorgeous girl in Osprey Falls. And I have to be careful, because if I so much as breathe on her dress too hard, her father will kill me.

We get to prom, pose under the flowered archway they have set up right when we walk in, and find a seat. I get a Pepsi for me and Al, Shirley Temples for Penny and Julie. Julie's wearing a bright green Cinderella dress with huge, poofy sleeves, which makes her, and our table, easy to spot as the ballroom fills up. We sit for a while and talk about *Tales From the Darkside: the Movie*, which just came out and Penny and I have seen, but Julie and Al have not. Dinner is served: undercooked steaks and overcooked potatoes, asparagus on the side and chocolate cake for dessert. None of us touches the asparagus, but we all finish the cake. We watch the other couples dance. Finally, Penny cajoles me out on the dance floor. They're playing "Wonderful Tonight" by Eric Clapton, so Penny and I wrap our arms around each other and sway, looking into each other's eyes. "I can't believe you're leaving me," she whispers, and I lean down to kiss her.

"You're fucking disgusting, Price," Bobby Foley slurs, pushing into me. Penny steps back, and I fall. I land on my hands and knees. Before I can decide whether or not to stay down or get up, Penny is helping me up, and as she does so, Bobby goes down, howling.

"What the—?" I ask, looking at him, then Penny. She shrugs and escorts me off the dance floor. She tells Al and Julie we're leaving, and they follow us out to the coat check. Penny stops to talk to Mr. Durden, who is one of the chaperones for the evening.

"Mr. Durden, I hate to get anyone in trouble, but I think Bobby Foley might be really drunk," she says timidly, looking at her history teacher with wide, innocent eyes. "He just fell on the dance floor, and I'm worried he's going to hurt himself." Mr. Durden scowls and strides towards Bobby, who is indeed still weak-kneed on the dance floor. We retrieve Julie's and Penny's coats and get to the car.

"What the hell just happened?" I ask.

"I didn't lie. Bobby is pretty pickled," Penny says, lighting a cigarette. "Couldn't you smell him?"

"So he really did just fall after he pushed me?" I press.

"Oh, my sweet, naive boyfriend," Penny says, stroking my cheek. "I might've accidentally punched him in the balls when I was helping you up. Can't say for sure," she adds, winking. I open the car door for her, and slide in after her.

"Okay," I say, grinning. "But you didn't wrinkle your dress when you did it, did you? Your father will kill me."

27.

With George out of state, I decide it's do-or-die time with Mom. Every morning, I brightly comment on how nice it is in the house without George around. Before she goes to work, I ask her if she's going to miss her friends at K-Mart. I remark that it's so relaxing to be able to sit at home without George's steel-toed boots there threatening to kick us around. Mom finally tells me to shut up.

"Knock it off, Curtis. We're moving. With George. The sooner you grow up and accept that, the better off we'll all be." The sides of her mouth turn down as she tells me this.

"Mom, honestly, why are you with him? He's not nice to you. He's an asshole. Was your wrist really a result of falling down the stairs? Did George do it?" The last question comes out as a whisper. I'm afraid of the answer.

Mom's eyes snap at me. "Curtis, my relationship with George is none of your business. You think this has been easy for me? Raising you two on my own, with no support from your father? I have no one here. *No one.* Sure, Marilyn Ewing has helped with you kids from time to time, but the way she looks down on me ... George is all I have. He's the only one that's been there for me. Who do you think paid the hospital bill after you fell out of the tree? That's right: George. How do you think I even had the money to chip in for half of your prom tux? So don't tell me he's an asshole, Curtis. He's pulled our butts out of the fire more times than I can count." She glares at me, and I shrink back. Mom walks out, headed to the Emerald, no doubt, and I can't help it: the tears start. When it comes down to it, my mother would choose her new husband over me. I'm trapped until I turn 18 and can get the hell away from both her and George.

The weeks are flying by too quickly. Penny and I keep bickering a lot, and Mom says it's a defense mechanism, to make it a little easier when we have to separate for good. I hate that we're fighting all the time, but I can't seem to stop myself. Penny dyes her hair orange, and I tell her she looks like a Dorito. She tells me I should consider washing my hair more because it looks like there's an oil slick on my head. I can't do this anymore. The day before I leave, we drive to Garrett Park together to look at the peacocks and swans, and we barely speak on the ride over.

Penny slams the door when she gets out of the truck and stalks over to the pond. A crowd of ducks immediately swims over to her, looking for stale bread. We'd picked up a bag of croutons before coming, and she shoves her fist in, throwing croutons like stones at the birds. I slink over next to her, waiting. This is it. Our last date together for a long, long time. I put my arm around her awkwardly. She sighs, and leans in a little towards me.

"This is hard," she says. "I don't want you to go."

"I don't want to go either!" I say. "It's not my fault!"

"I didn't *say* it was your fault, Curtis. Jesus! I'm trying to tell you I'm going to miss you. I love you, you asshole. Not so much lately, but I do."

I take her hand and guide her to a weathered bench next to the pond. The ducks are starting to surround us now, and Penny pushes a few to the side with her toe, getting an angry honk in response.

"I love you too, Penny. Uh … here, this is for you." I pull out Mr. Valley's delicate gold bookmark, carefully wrapped in tissue paper. Penny looks down at it for a moment, and her whole body shudders. She's crying, and I wrap her in my arms. We spend the rest of the afternoon sitting on the bench, looking out at the angry ducks. I try to memorize everything: the green algae on the pond; the curve of Penny's chin. I want to stay in this moment forever.

When dusk falls, we head back to the truck. Penny lies back in the cab, hitching her skirt up, pulling me down to her and kissing me sloppily. We manage a quickie before the ranger comes over to knock on the window and tell us the park is closing. We drive home in silence, Penny sniffling occasionally. When I pull into her driveway,

I take her hand; it's shaking. I kiss her goodbye for twenty minutes, and my heart sinks when she climbs out of the truck and heads for the front door, turning back to wave goodbye. Nothing will ever be the same again.

28.

I guess the house in Chesterbury is nice. It's a six-hour drive from Osprey Falls, and me and Sally ride in my truck, following Mom all the way down. Sally gets more and more animated as we drive, pointing out flowering trees and the sign for Cracker Barrel along the way. I get more and more quiet, missing Penny, hating Mom, wishing George would die. When we finally pull on to Tierney Street, the sun is starting to set, and when I follow Mom into the dirt driveway, a rabbit shoots into the bushes to avoid us. Rabbits. Bushes. Being able to look at the yard without seeing the yards of our neighbors next door. It's nice. But it isn't Osprey Falls.

I step out of the truck, stretching my legs. My jeans are stuck to my ass, sweaty from the long ride. I walk toward the back, checking out the yard. The grass is greener than a ball field, neatly mown. Trees surround the property, which Mom says is bordered by state land in back. Years ago, she explains, train tracks ran through this area, but after the tracks were abandoned, the state turned them in to walking paths. She calls them the airline trails, which makes no sense, but I don't want to argue with her. Arguing is all we've done since she announced the big move, and it's just plain worn me out.

There's a crabapple tree near the house, with a wooden bench swing hanging underneath, which is nice, especially since it faces out toward the woods.

The house itself is another story. It's a small ranch, painted bright yellow with orange shutters. It looks like a daffodil threw up on it. Mom is all smiles, showing us up the brick walk, unlocking the front door. She hands Sally and me our own house keys with a big flourish, like we've won some sort of prize in Hell.

A wall of stale cigar smoke hits us, a reminder that George got here first and has already marked his territory with his scent. The entryway has brown vinyl flooring that's supposed to look like patio stone, even though it's inside. To the left are two bedrooms directly across from each other, with a hall closet in between them. That will be Mom and George's bedroom to the left and Sally's room to the right. We start toward the other end of the house. Mom shows us the kitchen, which has light-green striped wallpaper and a red vinyl floor. The colors make me think of a dying Christmas tree, silently begging for water. I hate it immediately.

"New countertops," Mom brags, then opens up a door off of the kitchen. "This is your room, Curtis," she squeals. "You finally have your own room! We put you down this end of the house to give you a little space." The living room and bathroom are also off of the kitchen, so I don't know how much privacy I'm really going to have, but at least I'm out of the closet.

The first night in the house is the longest of my life. I toss and turn on my bed, which squeaks each time I move. I hear a dog howling in the distance, and someone gets up in the middle of the night to get a drink, because I can hear ice clinking on glass. Around three in the morning, I finally turn on my light and start reading the book Albert gave me as a going-away present, a biography on Stan Lee. I'm just about finished with it when I hear movement in the kitchen. I poke my head out and see Mom starting the coffee. I figure it's safe to get up now and pretend everything's just fine, even though it's not.

George has already started his new job, since he came up here weeks before us to get settled in. Now that we're in the same house together again, I'm finding it hard to hide how much I hate his guts. I don't bother speaking to him when I pass him on my way to the bathroom. When he shuffles around the kitchen to get a cup of coffee, I take my mug and go outside, settling on to the swing under the tree. I wait here until I hear the car door slam, signaling his departure for work.

I decide to explore the town. Chesterbury is pretty small, and if you take a left off our road, you pass about ten different white churches and a brick synagogue with ivy climbing up the sides.

There's a small ice cream stand right at the end of the road, and I can see a line forming, even though it's just after 10. I wonder if they were open at 3 a.m.?

I pass the elementary school and wind up at what seems to be the only traffic light in town. I take a right at yet another white church and find a pair of gas stations. Ironically, they are practically across the street from each other. I turn around at Ted's Market, apparently the only place in Chesterbury to buy groceries, and head back. It has taken me just three minutes to explore the whole town.

On the way back to the house, my eye catches a sign for a book sale, which I missed on the way down. Maybe one of the churches distracted me. I make a quick left in to the parking lot next to the sign. I have just found the local library. Salvation!

I wait for the doors to open, which isn't until 11. I go through my glove compartment, organizing it. I find an old straw wrapper and smooth it out, folding it carefully and putting it back in the glove box. It might be Penny's, left there after one of our trips to McDonald's for shakes.

Finally I can see a woman with black hair and wide hips approach the glass doors with a key in her hand. I make my way inside, a little nervous about being in a new library with a totally different layout from the one I know like the back of my hand in Osprey Falls. I take a few missteps, wind up in the children's section for one confused moment, but eventually I locate the fiction room. Many of the books are old, and I've read a lot of them, but I do find a Robert McCammon that I haven't read yet. I hold it to my chest like a consolation prize. I'm in a strange town in a strange state, but at least I have found one friend.

The librarian gives me a little bit of a problem because I don't have a Connecticut driver's license yet, but I explain to her that we just moved in to town, and if she wants, I can drive her to the house we just bought, and I'm so frantic that I think she feels bad for me. She issues me a temporary card and tells me to come back with my school record or license once I get it.

It's too early in the day to call Penny, so when I get home, I ask Sally if she wants to check out the airline trail. She's game, and changes into pink sweatpants, her freshly washed hair pulled back in a ponytail. I have to admit, this move was probably the best thing that could have happened to her. It's been a long time since I've seen my sister happy.

We walk gingerly down a small hill to the entrance of the airline trail. "It's so beautiful here," Sally says, humming, and I look at the cloudless sky, the dry lawns of our neighbors dotted with brown patches. There's a shattered beer bottle at the mouth of the airline path, littering the way with green glass. A glob that smells foul is near the start of the trail, and I squat to inspect it. It's a splayed frog, blackened, with a neat BB hole right through its soft belly.

Sally smiles as we start down, pointing out lady slippers and skunk cabbage in the marshy area by the side of the dirt path.

"How do you know what that stuff is?" I ask, because it's not like Osprey Falls was full of nature preserves.

"Girl Scouts," she shrugs, and I remember now. She was in Scouts up 'til fourth grade, until Mom couldn't really afford it any more. Sally had lost interest by that time anyway, more interested in MTV than merit badges, so I'm sure she didn't put up a fuss. I wonder if she regrets it now.

We stop about a half-mile down, where there's a bench and a water fountain. I'm sweating and panting. I start to glumly chalk it up to being out-of-shape, but decide to blame it on the warm weather instead. Sally sits next to me, pointing out some painted turtles sitting on a log in the middle of a swampy pond. A minute later, a short, blond-haired kid about our age jogs up, stops in front of Sally, and puts his hands on his knees, breathing hard.

"Got any room on that bench?" he asks. Sally slides over, and he sits down. His name is Charles but everyone calls him Doogie, because he looks like the guy on TV. Doogie will be a senior at CHAD this year, like me. He shakes my hand, but he's talking mostly to Sally, who's eating him up. She's smiling and giggling and, my God, I think she's flirting. It's kind of nice to see her bat her eyes at this little doofus.

Doogie works part-time at the market in town, and he knows that they're looking for cashiers; Sally should put in an application, you know, if she's looking for work. Maybe I'm looking for work, too, but Doogie doesn't mention anything about Ted's Market being in dire need of bag boys. Sally asks him if there's anything to do around town, and there isn't, though Doogie likes to hang out at the cemetery behind the congregational church on his lunch breaks and after school sometimes. Sally asks if that's where the local kids party, and he looks at her funny, a wrinkle forming between his two eyebrows like he's smelling something bad (and with all the dog shit along this path, it's a very real possibility) and says no, he just likes to hang out there because it's quiet, and he can walk among the tombstones and unwind. I think for sure Sally is going to laugh in his face and ask where the grown men hang out, but she just says it sounds nice and shyly reaches over, touching his hand. By the time we stand up to walk back up the trail, Doogie has gotten Sally's number, and he's walking home with us, so he can point out where he lives, which is just down a ways, over on Peppermill.

I call Penny as soon as I know she's home and tell her how much I hate it here in Chesterbury. "You've only been there a day and a half, Curtis," Penny says, and I can hear her smile through the phone. "Sounds like Sally's off to a good start," she adds, and the tears prick up in my eyes as Penny tells me about her day, and Mrs. Whitford, the new tenant at Sunny Brook. I don't belong here. I belong with my friends and my job and my library at Osprey Falls, not trapped in this disgusting daffodil house with Mom's bottles of vodka and George's stinking cigars and Sally's new dorky boyfriend.

Penny doesn't understand.

29.

I've taken to spending my days exploring and avoiding George. It's hard when he's home, drinking and practicing shooting beer cans in the back yard with the handgun he bought from some guy at work for "protection." I've seen deer, and some rabbits, and I think I spotted a skunk once, but no robbers or gangs of hoodlums, so I don't know what he's protecting us from. Mom wants me to plant a garden out back, but it's too late in the season to start, according to the lady I talked to down at the feed store in Gatlin. It turns out Gatlin, the next town over, is only five minutes down the road opposite from Chesterbury proper, and at least they have things like a real supermarket chain and a comic book store, TJ's. I spend forty dollars on a kick-ass bust of Venom that TJ had in his window, and now it sits alone on the one shelf I have in my bedroom. Venom is emerging from a pool of symbiote, black goo dripping off him, mouth open and full of needle-like teeth, howling as he emerges. George hates it, which only proves it's cool as hell.

The Venom statue is also a reminder that I'm getting low on funds, and I need a job, fast. Plus, if I want to see Penny, I'm going to need travel money. I certainly don't want to work at Ted's so I can watch Sally and Doogie make goo-goo eyes at each other all day. The Chesterbury librarian is no help, except she mentions as an afterthought that the library in Gatlin is looking for someone part-time to re-stack the returned books and do some dusting and cleaning. The woman in Gatlin eyes me nervously when I ask for an application. I have Mom trim my bangs and I make sure to be freshly showered and wearing a tie when I turn it back in. I'll admit I've been a little ripe lately, since there's no one here in Connecticut that I care about smelling nice for, but I figure for the library job, I'll make the effort. It takes a week for them to get back to me, but thanks to a glowing recommendation from Dottie when they call my references, I'm in. It's nice to have somewhere to go four days a week.

School's going to start soon, and I have to go for orientation a week before with all of the freshmen, even though I'll be a senior, because I'm new. CHAD has kids from a bunch of different towns, since Chesterbury, Hillcrest, Addison, and Dellford are all too small to support a high school in their own town. The school is four times as big as Osprey Falls High, since it's pulling in kids from four towns, and I have nightmares about getting lost on my first day.

Penny finally comes to visit the weekend before school is supposed to start, borrowing her father's car to drive down. Mom had to promise Mr. Paradise that she'd keep us separated. Penny has to stay with Sally in her room, and me in mine. True to her word, Mom is going to sleep in a chair in the kitchen, just to make sure no funny business goes on. It's kind of pointless, since George takes Mom to an exhibit at the civic center on Saturday, and Sally has to work, so Penny and I wind up alone in the house together for a good part of the day anyway. She still looks beautiful, even with her hair cut in a bob and dyed navy blue. As soon as she arrives, I hug her so hard I never want to let go. I breathe in deep, my heart cartwheeling at the scent of her, part Obsession by Calvin Klein, part baby-powder deodorant. We kiss for a while out in the driveway before I grab her overnight bag and bring her in to see the house.

Penny exclaims over the kitchen with its huge picture window overlooking the yard and its red tile. She tells Sally she loves what she's done with her room, which is painted light blue with sheer curtains, with photos of Billy Idol and Adam Ant taped around the mirror over her dresser. She checks out my room and slides her arm around my waist as she admires my stark walls and milk crates stuffed with Stephen King and Jack Ketchum. "No more closet for you, Curtis," she whispers and gives me a peck on the cheek. "This is nice. I didn't know what to expect after your phone calls, but I'm happy to see that this is … nice."

I shrug. It's a lot better now that Penny's here, but already a pit is forming in my stomach because I know she's going to have to leave in a couple of days.

30.

Penny and I explore together. We have sex in the cemetery, in the archives of the library, in the woods that border the backyard. She finds a tick crawling up her thigh after that last tryst and immediately nixes any return trips to the woods.

Our last morning together, she's packing her bags and rummaging through her suitcase. She pulls out some concert tees—AC/DC, Twisted Sister, Metallica.

"Here," she says, tossing them at me.

"What are these?" I can't remember ever listening to Twisted Sister. Did I forget some sort of special song? Had we once made sweet, sweet love to the tune of "We're Not Gonna Take It?"

"You're going to need an image, Curtis," she says, brushing my cheek with her perfectly manicured blue nails. "You go into a new school anywhere, you're going to get chewed up and spit out if they even get a hint of what a sensitive soul you are. It's not a bad thing," she adds when she sees my scowl. "It's just how it is. You need to create an identity. You'll be the bad boy. The quiet, bad boy," she smiles and gives me a quick kiss. "Wear these with your jeans. Your hair's just long enough to pull it off—but I'd let it grow a little longer, if I were you. Just be careful. You know how all the girls dig the bad boys."

I murmur some words of love, and we're in the middle of a heavy petting session when Mom yells that it might be time for Penny to hit the road if she wants to make it back to Maine before dark. My heart breaks as I wave goodbye from the front door. I stop speaking to Mom and George for a week, not that they notice. It's their fault I'm here and not with Penny.

I wake up with a stomachache the first day of school. I'm mad at myself—what am I, eight? I jerk off, pretending my hand is Penny's lips, and feel a little better.

I pull into the lot where they told us at orientation it was okay for seniors to park. I'm wearing Penny's Metallica shirt, with jeans and my beat-up Converse All Stars. Her costume works miracles. Nobody talks to me, though I get a few looks. But there's no Connecticut version of Bobby Foley waiting to kick my ass between classes, either. During my free period toward the end of the day, I get a stroke of genius. There's a skinny kid with long, bleach-blond hair relaxing in the smoking section outside. He's wearing a Poison tee and a bandanna, like he's hoping he'll get discovered as the perfect replacement for Bret Michaels as front man for the band. In my old school, he'd be labeled a poser and get kicked around occasionally by the football team. Here, he seems to be respectfully ignored. I stroll over to him and ask him casually for a cigarette.

"Sure, man," he says lazily, digging in to his pocket. "They're Reds, hope that's okay."

"That's my brand, man," I say, giving him a nod. He hands me one and offers a lighter.

"I'm Curtis," I say, lighting up. *Please don't let me cough, Lord*, I pray, but I manage to pull it off, inhaling slowly.

"Corona," he says, tucking the lighter back into his pocket. "Where you from?"

I put my back against the brick wall he's leaning against and slide down. I guess I'm a smoker now.

31.

I usually meet Corona—which, it turns out, is his last name, not his first, which is a bit of a relief that his parents aren't nuts or hardcore alcoholics—in the parking lot before school. A tall, heavy kid named Eric often joins us there as well, and we smoke a few butts and complain about the stuck-up bitches in town before heading in to class. Eric has bad acne on his cheeks and chin, and he's trying to grow a beard to help cover it up, but it's been coming in pretty splotchy so far. Corona and I have taken to calling him Sasquatch, but never to his face because he could kick both of our asses without breaking a sweat.

I'm doing okay, I guess, but Mom isn't. I usually head to the library most afternoons, and by the time I get home from my shift a little past six, Mom is already half in the bag. She usually remembers to cook, but she doesn't eat with Sally and me, just shuts herself up in her room with the TV going. George doesn't come home for dinner at all, which is good, because when he *is* home, he's usually screaming at Mom. Sometimes I think I hear him slap her, but when I jump out of my room, fists curled, she tells me everything's fine and to butt out. Occasionally Doogie comes over, but not until Mom's safely in her room, then he and Sally giggle and whisper and disappear into Sally's bedroom for a few hours. She better watch out; I know she wants to be a good girl here in Connecticut where her reputation can't follow her, but she's going to wind up pregnant again. When I mention this to her, she gives me a cold, steely look, then she tells me that even though it's none of my business, she's on the pill. I know she hates telling me that, but it does make me feel a little better.

At night, I hear Mom stumbling around. Her trips to the bathroom get more frequent the later it gets. The last visit of the night is the one where she pukes. I can hear her in there, gagging and vomiting; I think she's making herself do it so she doesn't die of alcohol poisoning in her sleep. She's never up the next morning by the time I leave for school. Neither is George, which is a relief.

He's been acting weird lately. Usually he tells us about upcoming stuff at the civic center, but he hasn't mentioned anything for a month now, and one day on my way to the library after school, I see his truck at the Howling Dog in Gatlin, instead of at work where he should be.

And when Mom and George are both home and awake at the same time, they just yell at each other until I have to leave the house before I kill him. I don't think I could, though, which is the most frustrating thing—I just have to sit there with clenched fists and listen to him telling my mother what a useless bitch she is, and I can't do a thing about it. He's stronger than me, plus, Mom will just take his side anyway. George has singlehandedly ruined our lives, dragging us to Connecticut, away from Penny and Albert, to this godforsaken place where Mom has become a drunk, and Sally is making the same old mistakes. Corona and Eric are all right, but it's not home.

I hate George, and I hate it here.

I've written a couple of letters and called Albert a few times, but I can tell the friendship is fading fast. His chemistry lab partner this year is Danny Evans, and whenever I call Al he's either with Danny or telling me about their Dungeons and Dragons games. It's pretty lame. I guess when I was there, Albert didn't seem like such a loser, but now that we have some space between us, he looks like a total nerd. I'm pretty sure if Corona and Eric ever met him, they'd beat the crap out of him and then kick me in the ribs a few times for good measure just for ever talking to Al. Best to let that friendship cool, I guess.

32.

On Friday night, about fifteen minutes before my shift is scheduled to end at the library, Ms. Lacoss asks me to alphabetize the movies. I might grumble about this on any other night, but Corona and Eric are at Lake Compounce for a Tesla concert, so I don't really have any plans for the evening. I organize the VHS tapes, borrow *Dead Poets Society* to watch later, and get out around seven. I decide to do a quick loop through Gatlin to see if anything interesting is going on in town before heading home. George's truck is once again parked outside of the Howling Dog, even though Mom said just this morning that he was working late, handling security for some big Titanic exhibit at the civic center. What the hell? Clearly something's up, and I'm worried that something's wrong with Mom that made him leave work early. I decide to go in.

The Howling Dog is dimly lit and smoky, smelling of stale beer and cigarettes. It's crowded, but most of the people are gathered around faded green pool tables, holding weathered pool cues and watching a slow game unfold. I spot George hunched over the bar, an ashtray holding what appears to be the butt of one of his cigars propped in front of him. He's sitting next to a thin woman with bedraggled hair that, had it been washed and combed, might have been brown.

"George," I say, approaching. He jumps, startled. The scraggly woman looks up at me and offers a smile, revealing a gummy maw absent of teeth.

"What the fuck you doin' here?" George growls. The toothless lady shakes her head, looking down into her beer again.

"I could ask the same of you," I shoot back. "Is Mom okay? I thought you were working tonight. Some big exhibit?"

"They can handle it themselves," he says, then: "Your mother's right at home where she should be. Don't you question me. You still have a roof over your head, right? Fucking spoiled ingrate."

I decide to take another tack. "Are you coming home any time soon? I'm on my way now; I could tell Mom when you expect to be there."

This touches a nerve, but I don't know why. "Don't you tell your whore of a mother a fucking thing!" he shouts, standing. Although I now have about an inch on him, it still feels like he's towering over me, threatening. His meaty fist is drawn back, and even though his words are slurred, I'm guessing any punch he throws would land close to target, so I shrink back.

"Jesus, George, calm down! I won't tell her anything, okay? What the fuck?"

"Get out!" he roars, and I spin around to leave, wanting to get away before he goes for my throat again, like he did that one time at the dinner table.

"Fuck, George, you haven't told them you lost your job yet?" I hear the woman say in a low smoker's voice.

Oh, fuck.

Self-preservation makes me keep walking, hoping he thinks I didn't hear. My whole body is tense, and I try not to walk too fast, but the sense of needing to escape is too much, and I'm practically jogging to the exit. I turn to look back at George, and his cold, dead eyes are locked on mine. He's scowling.

If I can get back to the house, talk to Mom, convince her to leave … then I can get back home, to Penny. Mom will have to take my side now. George lost his job, and he's been hiding it from Mom. I break a couple of traffic laws in my race to get home. I call out for Mom as soon as my feet hit the fake stone linoleum in the entryway; she doesn't respond. Sally and Doogie are in Sally's room, fooling around. I have to wonder if Mom can hear them—her room is right across the hall, for chrissakes—and just doesn't care anymore.

"Mom!" I call out again, impatient.

I hear shuffling in her bedroom, so I move toward her door and knock. She opens the door, and I can tell she's drunk, probably plastered by now. Her hair is a tangled mess and her worn face looks mealy and sagged; I can see hard lines on either side of her mouth, around her eyes, and creasing her forehead. She's wearing a stained sweatshirt that was once peach-colored before many trips through the wash, and sweatpants that are too big and have a hole in the knee. Jesus, when did this happen to her? A memory of Mom and Nana at our kitchen table in Osprey Falls jumps before my eyes, Mom looking young, laughing and relaxed. They'd been playing Scrabble, and Nana had been winning. *Roon isn't a word, you old cheater*, Mom had said, but Nana had just sipped her coffee. *Are you daring to call your mother a liar, young lady?* Nana had replied.

Yes, that's right, I confirm to myself. *Mom was a young lady then.* Not this gnarled, sad creature in front of me now.

"Wha?" she asks, waiting for me to explain why I'd interrupted her drunken repose.

"Mom, it's George. He's at the bar in Gatlin right now. He lost his job! I don't know how long it's been. I've seen his Scout there a few times in the past couple of weeks. Maybe a month." The words come out in a rush.

"What'cha mean? He's been goin' to work," Mom says, not comprehending.

"Mom, listen to me. George *hasn't* been going to work, that's what I'm saying. He lost his job. He's been lying to you. To all of us. We have to get out of here. I saw him at the bar, and he's pissed."

In my mind, I've been thinking about the next step. If George doesn't have a job, then there's no reason to stay here in Chesterbury. We can pack up now, before George gets home, and be out of here in an hour. Leave Connecticut and George behind. Go back to Osprey Falls; to Penny. My heart leaps.

"Outta here?" Mom's eyes clear for a moment. "Curtis, what kind of nonsense are you talking 'bout?"

I take a deep breath and try to be patient. "Mom, George is an asshole. He's hit you before, and he'll do it again." She recoils, as if it's my words that have struck her. I decide to barrel on. "I'm guessing you only stayed with him because he was paying the bills. That's what I'm telling you. He *can't* pay the bills anymore. He doesn't have a job. And he's a liar. He's a bully and a liar, and we don't need to stay with him anymore."

Mom looks at me sadly. "Curtis, iss not that easy. I'm sure George has his reasons for keepin' thissa secret, and I *am* going to talk to him 'bout it. But I really have no choice. He's dunna lot for us over the years. I can't just leave him." She sounds a *little* more articulate now, as if the news that her husband has been deceiving her about where he's been going every day has helped sober her up a little.

My face turns red. "Mom, the first time we met George, you told him I was the man of the house and could take care of our family. That's what I'm trying to do! Let's pack up and get the hell out. We don't need George. I'll get a job and support us."

Mom shakes her head. "Curtis, 'm tired, and you're talking nonsense. Plus, I still havva deal with George when he gets home. We can talk 'bout this later." She shuts the door, leaving me in a hot steam of frustration in the hallway.

Sally pokes her head out of her room. "What's going on?" she asks.

"George lost his job and didn't tell Mom, or any of us, for that matter. I think we should leave before he comes home. Let him find a new family." I look at her hopefully.

"Right now? Doogie and I are watching *Return of the Jedi*. Yoda just died." She sniffs at me and closes her bedroom door again, as if my request is completely ridiculous in the face of a Muppet death scene.

Well, fuck that. I'll pack first, then *make* Mom leave. Sally, too. Doogie can come with us for all I care; I just want out.

I try calling Penny to let her know what's going on, but Mr. Paradise informs me that she's not home yet from her shift at Sunny Brook. I go into my room and look around. I don't have much to pack. I grab a couple of black garbage bags from the kitchen and come back in. My jeans, T-shirts, shoes, and a copy of *Watchers* by Dean Koontz that I haven't finished yet go into the bag. It's a library book, but I can mail it back to Ms. Lacoss after I finish it. I'd drop it off on our way out of town, but it's really good, and I don't want to stop reading it halfway through.

I hear the front door open. It must be George. I'd been hoping he wouldn't come home this quickly. I poke my head out of my room. Sally better hope he doesn't check in on her, or she and Doogie are in big trouble. The rule is *supposed* to be no guests in the bedroom unless the door stays open.

It's George, all right. He's weaving a little; I halfheartedly hope he'll pass out on the couch so we can be on our way without him interfering. I step backwards quietly, closing my door as softly as possible. I don't want him to hear me packing and take it upon himself to investigate.

I open a second garbage bag and throw in notes from Penny, the two letters I've gotten from Albert since moving, and a picture of Penny that I took that last day at the park together before I moved. She looks sad in the photo; the sun's setting behind her delicate face, and her cheek is in shadow. Mom had gotten me a cheap frame for it at a yard sale, and I'd kept it by my bed so I could look at it every night. Now, maybe in just six hours, I'd be with her again. I wouldn't leave her this time, either.

Mom's screeching from down the hall shakes me out of my reverie. Apparently she's decided to confront George right now. Shit. I was hoping she'd let him be, just to lull him into a false sense of security until we get the hell out. I toss the framed photo in the bag and open my closet to pull out the clothes that are hanging there. No time to get sentimental. We have to go.

George calls Mom a drunken, useless bitch, and my fingernails dig in to the flesh of my palms. She wouldn't drink if it wasn't for him. He drove her to this, took her away from everything she knew and could count on in Osprey Falls, and dumped her in the middle of nowhere. Mom has no friends here. Only the guy at the liquor store knows her by name. I hear a thud and a feminine-sounding groan. He's fucking beating her! That's it; I've had it.

I look around for a weapon, something I can knock George out with right after I tell him what a gigantic piece of shit he is. I lean into my closet; I think my old baseball bat is in here somewhere, the one Nana gave me for my sixth birthday. That's when the gunshots start.

It's one at first, then a pause; after a few seconds, two more. What the—? It's George, it must be, and he's shooting at Mom. Oh my God, what if he hit her? That fucking sonofabitch—I'll kill him! I'll fucking tear his head off—I don't care if he's stronger than me. I quickly give up my search for the bat and grab the heaviest thing I can see, my awesome Venom statue. I've had it with this asshole. I can sneak up on him while he's shooting up the room and knock him out; he's probably so drunk that he won't even hear me coming. I hope that fucker doesn't get a shot off at me before I bash his brains in, but if he does, I hope it's in the gut; I think people survive gut shots. Fuck it. I'm going in.

I step out to the hallway and don't hear a thing. Where is everyone? As quickly and quietly as I can, I make my way down the other end of the house, where Mom's and Sally's rooms are. I stop outside Mom's door and peek in. For a moment, the blood stops pumping in my veins.

What's left of Mom is splayed half-on, half-off the bed. Her throat is shredded, but her head lolls back, and she's staring wide-eyed at the ceiling. It almost looks like she's smiling, a hideous grin, and her dirty peach sweatshirt is now stained with blood. For one ridiculous moment I think, *is that real?* My breath is gone, which is good, I suppose, because if I scream, George will hear me. George, the murderer. I whirl around to get to Sally and Doogie. The door to Sally's room is open now, and I spot, out of the corner of my eye, a glimpse of two bodies on the floor.

George has gotten them. He's going to try for me now.

Without thinking, I run back to my room and shut the door. I don't know where George is, but I can see through the window that his Scout is still outside. Can I crawl out of this little window? Is there time to get the glass up, punch out the screen, and squeeze through? The floorboards creaking in the hallway tell me I'm out of time. I have to hide.

I dive in to the safest place I can think of—the closet. I've spent more time in a closet than out, it seems, and now I need to hide, dig down, disappear; thank God I didn't have time to pull out my clothes and pack them. I start pulling them down off the hangers and over me, trying to cover myself up, as quietly as possible. I'm pretty sure—yes, I'm hidden now, and hopefully he'll forget about me, he'll leave in his rage, and then I can go take care of Mom, get her some help. Why hadn't I taken the EMT class yet? What had been so important that I didn't get that done? I'm a fucking idiot. If I'd taken the class, maybe I could save my family now.

Time crawls, and I realize I've been holding my breath; I exhale as quietly as I can, but I want to gasp, gulp for air. I clamp a hand over my mouth and force myself to stay calm, to count in my mind as I breathe—inhale, one two three, exhale, one two three. My other hand still clutches Venom, in case I need to use him to club my way to freedom.

I can't believe this is happening. Who is this fucking madman? How could Mom marry him? Mom—her glassy eyes staring up at the ceiling, the blood on her shirt. Was she faking being dead so George would leave her alone? Maybe that's it. Mom's always been good in an emergency; she's not really dead. And Sally. All she wanted was a fresh start in a new place. To leave her past behind. She seemed happy here, even when I was trying to get her to join me in my pity party; it's not fair. Fucking George. He's fucked up everything for all of us.

I don't hear anything. Maybe George left. Could I have missed the door opening, the sound of his exit? I'll wait for a few minutes more and then take a look around. If I can get out of the house, get to my truck, I'll drive right to the police station. Where are my keys? I slowly move my hand down to my pocket, feel the hard metal of my car keys, right where they should be. Salvation.

It's so quiet. He must have left. Dare I breathe?

"Hello, Curtis," George growls, pulling Nana's old sweater off my face and drawing a bead on my forehead with his handgun. His eyes are wild, and blood spatters his cheeks and chest. I'm looking at a madman.

33.

If you'd asked me what I might guess my last thoughts would be, I would have said that I'd be thinking about Penny, and how much I love her, our first date at the cemetery when she kissed me or our last date in Maine at the duck pond. The soft angles of her cheeks or the way her eyes flash when she's excited or mad. Her kisses, quick and sweet when she lingers before going in to her father's house, urgent and hard when we're having sex. I would have said that my last moments would be filled with my very first love.

But I am an ordinary boy. And the last name in my mind, the one that never makes it to my lips, is simple:

Mom!

34.

I am here but not here. Everywhere and nowhere. Energy, but not mass.

Nobody is here with me. I am alone.

George marches through the house, his stupid comb-over sticking up in long strands. I follow him, screaming at him, calling him every horrible name I can think of, but he doesn't hear me. When he stops to glance in my bedroom, I understand why. There's my body, curled in the closet. I'm dead. That rotten motherfucker has killed me. This gives me pause, and I settle at my door for a moment. George grabs a six-pack of beer out of the refrigerator, and a while later, it registers in my mind that a car has driven off.

I move down to Mom's room, see her cold, gaping smile, still unmoving, still staring, and look away. Where *is* Mom now? I mean, I'm here, so shouldn't she be? I call out for her and get no response. I don't know how this whole dead thing works. Maybe she's off playing cards with Nana somewhere.

I peek in on Sally and Doogie. Their bodies are on the floor, Doogie face-up, eyes wide in terror. Sally is face down, one arm draped over Doogie's chest. There's blood matted in the hair on the back of her head and a deep red stain on Doogie's Bart Simpson T-shirt. The shirt reads "Don't have a cow, man." Good advice.

I don't sense Sally or Doogie here either. Where the hell is everyone? I'm starting to feel like everyone had plans to meet up after our deaths and forgot to mention it to me. I decide to wait.

Our bodies would've lain in the house indefinitely, if not for Doogie. While we're all new to town, with few connections, Doogie has lived in Chesterbury all of his life. He has a routine. While I'm sitting on my bed, trying to wrap my mind around what's happened and trying to figure out what's next, I hear Doogie's dad outside our daffodil house, bellowing for Doogie to get his ass outside. When he pounds on the front door and gets no response, he's so furious he starts stalking the outside of the house, looking into windows, cursing out his son all the while. "Grounded for a month," he shouts. "Never going to be allowed out with Sally again," he bellows. He pushes his face against the window of Mom's room, and it takes him a moment for him to register what he is seeing.

What he sees is a nightmare.

When the police arrive, all of the steam has gone out of Doogie's dad. He's peered in through the rest of the windows, and he has a good idea of what's waiting. The police break down the front door, cautiously stepping past me, not seeing me, as I wait to greet them. I wander outside and see two burly officers holding Doogie's dad back gently but firmly as he wails, insisting that his son needs him.

George's Scout is in the driveway, but my truck is missing. A little detective work and the police realize that George probably fled in my Chevy. Figures. I'd filled the tank Friday morning, so the sonofabitch was escaping on my dime. I can't believe the nerve! I'm so angry I feel like I'm evaporating in to steam—I could kill George, that sonofa—and suddenly, I'm in my truck, sitting next to the cigar-chomping fiend as he crosses the state line into Maine. Where is he *going*? I look at George, sweat pouring off his face, flinching every time a car passes him, maybe worried it's the cops. I look back at the road. I think—yes, I'm sure of it—the old bastard is heading back to Osprey Falls. I try to take the wheel, to crash him into a semi that passes him on the left, but my hand whistles through the wheel and down to George's crotch. Disgusting. I sit back, useless arms tightly crossed, and wait for him to get us home. I let loose with a stream of curse words as he drives, but he seems to hear none of them. "Well, this is pointless," I announce. "Boo. Boooo," I add. George doesn't respond. So much for haunting him.

Our old house sits vacant; it looks like the landlord has been renovating it before renting it out again. They haven't changed the

locks, though, and George uses his old key to get in. He locks the
door behind him and begins muttering to himself: "Get money, get
alcohol, get out." He curses when he tries the sink and finds the water
is turned off. He still has dried blood still spattered on his face, neck,
arms, and clothing. I'm sure he wants to rinse off before going out in
the daylight. He paces, muttering to himself that all of this is Mom's
fault, he wouldn't have had to do what he did if she hadn't threatened
to leave him. Who did she think she was? And Sally and I, rotten
little ingrates, spoiled little shits, we'd had it coming. Didn't respect
his authority, his position as man of the house. None of this would've
happened if we'd just given him time to get his shit together, find
another job. He paces maniacally, mutters incoherently. Eventually,
he collapses in a corner, curling up, cradling his gun beside him like
a teddy bear.

I try kicking him. No dice. I poke my head outside, shout for
help, even though I know it's pointless. I brighten at the sight of my
truck, which George has parked right out front, not bothering to
hide it. *Maybe . . .* he can't get away. That would be just too supremely
unfair.

A little while later, I spot a police cruiser down by Bobby Foley's
house, first one, then another. My heart soars. They're coming.
I glance back inside at George, still snoring softly, our blood still
sticking to his skin. The Maine state police creep up to the house
silently, using hand motions to signal to each other, surrounding
the duplex. George stirs, rolls over, and continues his slumber. He
seems to hear nothing until the door slams open. He sits up, looking
confused. They arrest him without incident, haul him off to the
county jail, and put up crime scene tape. My truck still sits in the
driveway, where Penny Paradise spots it, her face lighting up, then
clouding when she sees the police tape.

35.

Penny had mentioned on the phone that she often strolls through my old neighborhood. She says some of her favorite memories are here, tucked inside the community center building or descending like the fading sunlight across the abandoned baseball field. She always glances at my house, looking to catch a glimpse of some forgotten moment: a joke we shared on the front porch or a stolen kiss as we looked for four-leaf clovers in the backyard. I grin and break out into a full run when I see her but pass right through her. *Fuck*. I turn and watch her as she studies the house. When she sees my truck, her eyes scan the porch quickly, perhaps wondering if I have returned to her. But the police tape is all wrong, out of place in this dusty, worn section of town. There's an officer stationed outside the house, and she approaches him.

"What's going on?" she asks, eyes widening. Her voice is pleading.

"This doesn't concern you, miss. Move along, please." He barely looks at her as he brushes her off.

"Please. My boyfriend used to live here. What's happening? Is Curtis okay?"

The officer looks more interested now. He asks Penny for her name and radios in to dispatch with the information. "Yes," the dispatcher informs him. "We'd like to talk to her. Can you bring her down to the station for questioning?"

Penny starts to sweat. She lights a cigarette and keeps asking what's going on. The policeman assures her that he'll answer her questions downtown. He signals to a female officer who has been lurking inside the duplex, tells the other cop he's escorting this young woman to the station. The female officer furrows her brow in concern, offers to be the one to escort Penny. The first officer shakes his head, assures his partner that he's got this. He turns back to Penny. How old is she? They'll need to talk to her parents, too. Okay, her father, then. "What's the best way to reach him, miss?"

Penny starts to cry. She manages to choke out her father's phone number at work between sobs. The officer puts a heavy arm around her shoulders to comfort her. "There, there," he says. "You'll be okay. Your father will meet you at the station, and you'll be all right. We should go." He pivots her toward a police car parked a few doors down the road. "You'll be all right," he echoes again.

Penny is not all right. I hover over her, helpless, wanting to let her know I'm okay, that I'm here, but I can't. She sits on an unforgiving metal bench at the police station for an hour until her father arrives. Once he gets there, she tells him what she knows, which is nothing except that my truck is back at my old house and there's police tape everywhere. Mr. Paradise goes into Papa Bear mode. Why is his daughter being held? What's going on here? Is she being charged with something?

A man and a woman, both graying, both in dark pant suits, escort Mr. Paradise and Penny and me into a room. It's not at all like the interrogation rooms I've seen on *Miami Vice*. It's more like the principal's office at school, which I've only seen once, when I cut class to hang out with Penny. In a soft voice, the female detective explains that they're investigating a case regarding George Jervis, my stepfather. They ask Penny when the last time she talked to me was. She answers in a quiet voice that she talked to me Thursday night, but adds that she tried to call me yesterday and today. I haven't called back. Am I okay?

The detectives exchange a glance. "I talked to Curtis on Friday, probably about 8 o'clock," Mr. Paradise offers. Penny shoots him a puzzled look.

"You did? Why didn't you tell me?" She frowns.

"You weren't home from work yet, and I didn't want you calling him back so late at night," Mr. Paradise sighs. I suspect he's been trying to get his daughter to cool off our relationship ever since I moved, but his eyes look hangdog now. It wouldn't have done much harm to let his daughter talk to me, even if it was late. There's the tiniest of tremors in his hands, and I think he's starting to suspect that there's some bad news coming. His daughter is going to be hurt. Maybe devastated.

"Has something happened to Curtis?" Penny asks, voice shaking. "Why won't you tell me what's going on?"

The female detective uses the same soothing tone to respond. "Penny, I'm sorry to have to tell you this, but yes, something's happened. The case we're investigating in conjunction with the Connecticut state police is a quadruple homicide. We believe one of the victims was Curtis Price. George Jervis is our prime suspect at the moment, and we have him in custody."

Penny gasps, then lets out a long, low moan. Her whole body slumps, folds into itself, as if she no longer has the strength to sit upright. She crosses her arms as if to hug herself and starts to rock. Her father clumsily wraps his arms around her shoulders, trying to bring her in for a comforting hug, but he's hampered by the chairs they both still sit in.

Okay, my life wasn't great, but my worst moments with George weren't as bad as this. To see this beautiful woman, *my* woman, the girl I love, in so much pain, and to not be able to comfort her, tell her I'm here? This is worse than being shot. This is tearing at my soul.

Mr. Paradise opens his mouth to ask a question, maybe get more details, to learn what, exactly, has happened, but he shakes his head and doesn't ask. His daughter is in no shape to hear more. He asks them if it's okay for him to take his daughter home and answer any other questions they might have later. The detectives nod, and he puts his arm around Penny's waist, helping her up. She is slumped against him as he practically carries her out to his car. I follow.

When they get home, Penny haltingly suggests that Albert should be called. She says she'll do it, but when she dials the number and he answers, she starts crying again and can't get the words out. Mr. Paradise gently takes the receiver from Penny's trembling hands and quietly explains to Al what has happened.

Within thirty minutes, Al and Julie are at the Paradise house, sitting on Penny's bed with her. Al's mother sends along a couple of

Valium pills for Penny. Penny refuses to take them, but later on, Mr. Paradise crushes one of them and mixes it into his daughter's tea.

Penny can't seem to stop weeping, though I can see her struggle to try. She and Al talk about George, recounting in detail every single time they can recall him being a total asshole.

"He kicked me out of the house one time, called me a tramp," Penny sniffles. "Just because Curtis had his arm around me when we were sitting on the couch. I was wearing a turtleneck that day, too. I remember wondering how in the name of God could a girl in a turtleneck be considered a tramp. I hated him so much that day," she recalls. "It was just an unfair thing to say."

"At least you were allowed over there," Al says, frowning. "We were best friends, but I was never allowed to go over his house. I think I went over there maybe twice all the time we were friends. Curtis told me his stepfather said he didn't want any of Curtis' friends coming over and messing up the place, eating all his food." Al is crying now, and Julie rubs his arm. "What a fucking worm! What kind of asshole doesn't want his kids to have any friends?"

"*Step*kids," Julie corrects him gently, and Penny offers her a grateful smile.

I cringe a little as I listen to the conversation. Had it really been such a big deal to not let Al see how we lived? What would've happened? I'm sure he would've still been my friend. I remember being ashamed that my bedroom was just a mattress in a closet. Would he have cared? He might have pitied me. Okay, yup, that would've been bad. I'm glad he blames George.

Mr. Paradise knocks on the bedroom door well after the sun has set. The three teenagers have been speculating on when the funerals will be and who might show up. He suggests that it might be time for Al and Julie to go. Julie nods, but Al's eyes go wide. He's not sure he can face his parents' tomb of a house tonight; not tonight, he says. Mr. Paradise calls Al's parents. His mother states that she's quite concerned Albert might use this little tragedy as an excuse to not study for his geometry exam scheduled for Thursday. Mr. Paradise tells Al's mother that her son will be staying over the Paradise house tonight so that he can go to grief counseling tomorrow with Penny.

He hangs up and shakes his head. I agree, Mr. P.: Al's parents aren't the type to solve problems with a handgun, certainly, but just the same, it doesn't mean they're any good at parenting.

Mr. Paradise drives Julie home, returns to the house, and readies the couch with sheets, pillows, and a comforter for Al. He crushes the Valium into Penny's tea, and checks her room later, cocking his head and listening to her breathe. He spends his night drinking coffee at the kitchen table, occasionally offering company each time Al restlessly comes to the table between bouts of fitful sleep.

I take this opportunity to fully check out the Paradise house. After all, my experiences there were limited to the living room couch, where Penny and I would sometimes watch a movie, Mr. Paradise hovering nearby like a sentinel guarding his daughter's chastity, and the kitchen table, where he'd delivered his effective pre-prom speech. I snoop around. Mr. P's bedroom is dark and bare; what appears to be an office with a big oak desk is in the room next door. I look at the glass display cases that line one wall. Wait a minute. Mr. Paradise clearly collects baseball cards, not guns. He'd *bluffed* me! We totally could've done it after prom. I laugh. His bluff had worked, at least on prom night, anyway, so I guess it was well played. I move back to the kitchen and sit at the table, worrying about Penny. I'm sure that's what Mr. P is doing, so we might as well do it together.

In the morning, Mr. Paradise phones the school to let them know that Penny and Al will be out that day. He calls out of work and sets about trying to help his daughter make it through the day.

36.

Penny hasn't gotten out of bed, and I'll admit it's really hard watching her suffer, plus I'm a little bored. I start thinking about Corona and Eric, and CHAD, wondering if anyone's heard about us yet, and sure enough, I find myself suddenly near my school locker. It appears that the CHAD students are only working with half the story: From the hallway chatter, I gather that people know only that Doogie, Sally and I have been killed, shot by some guy, maybe a jealous boyfriend of Sally's. I find Corona and Eric in their usual spot in the smoking area when two girls walk by, gossiping about the story.

"Dude, what did that chick just say? Was someone shot?" Eric starts up, puts out his cigarette on the brick wall behind him, and catches up to Emily Lonergan, the girl who'd been talking. He asks her what the scoop is, and when she tells him, explaining that Doogie Bennett was one of the victims, along with that new kid Curtis from Maine. The color drains from Eric's face.

"Curtis Price? The kid with the shaggy hair that always hangs out with me and Corona out here?" he asks gravely. Emily gulps, then bursts into tears. Her friend apologizes to Eric and rubs Emily's back as Eric tries to get more details out of her. She's crying hysterically, in loud, gasping sobs, and Eric gives up and walks with heavy steps back to Corona. He tells Corona what he's learned, and the two of them sit, looking shell-shocked. They ignore the bell signaling the start of school, and continue chain-smoking outside for the whole day. Corona announces that he blames himself for not getting an extra ticket to Tesla so I could go with them that night. If I'd been with them at Lake Compounce, sneaking beers and riding the kiddie rides, cruising for chicks and waiting for the concert to start, none of this would've happened.

Eric admits he feels bad, terrible really, but there's not much that can be done now. Plus, he's managed to peek through his haze of shock long enough to realize that a crowd is developing around them. It seems like every kid who ever had a class with me, every girl who ever smiled at me in the hallway, has decided that they should converge at the smoking area. I had no idea I was so popular. Emily Lonergan comes by after third period and apologizes to Eric again, eyes full of tears. By the end of the day, she's sitting between his legs, leaning back against his chest, sharing his cigarette. The whole thing sucks, Eric acknowledges to Corona in a whisper, but he's sure I wouldn't hold it against him if he manages to score a little pussy out of this whole experience.

I don't hold it against him. But it does remind me that I'd always liked Corona just a little bit more than him.

Time to check in at my old school. Over at Osprey Falls High, there are more tears, more wailing, more grief-stricken, traumatized students. After all, Sally and I grew up here and knew these kids all our lives. They only know that Sally and I are dead, and that the murderer fled to their own pristine, lily-white suburb to escape capture. A mass murderer in Osprey Falls? What is the world coming to? Though he *was* captured in The Meadows, which explains a lot—that *is* the trashy side of town, after all. I stroll through the hallways, amazed. For the first time in my life, everyone is talking about me. They sound almost upset. By midafternoon, an announcement is broadcasting over the loudspeaker that grief counselors will be available for anyone who needs to meet with them. As I flit from classrooms to hallways, it seems like just about everyone in school has a story about me or Sally.

These are the same kids that ignored and shunned me for eleven years. How is it that they're all suddenly my best friends? And Sally, who was called every dirty name in the book by these same catty, mean girls who are now weeping in the hallways, mascara running?

For a moment, I wish she were here with me, just so I could hear what she'd hurl in their general direction. I miss Sally. I hope she is okay.

I turn the corner and see a familiar figure. Stinky Pinky I did—do—actually know. She's shrinking into her locker this Monday morning, clearly trying not to be noticed. It's a posture I'm familiar with: I perfected it. She blinks when Mr. Wild approaches her. This is unusual. The other students torment her, and the teachers largely ignore her, even when the tormenting is going on. He asks her delicately to step into the empty classroom down the hall with him. She trembles, probably thinking she's in trouble, but meekly follows him. Pinky glances at her copy of *The Complete Dorothy Parker* still clutched in her hands and murmurs, "What fresh hell is this?"

Mr. Wild has collected some of the other Meadows kids: Peggy Ewing and Bobby Foley are already slouched in the classroom. Mr. Wild is gentle as he tells them the news, that Sally and I are dead, murdered by our stepfather. Pinky shakes her head as he continues on about how they can meet with the school guidance counselor if they need to, or maybe he could call their parents if they want to go home for the day. Pinky speaks quickly, trying to get the words out all at once. "Remember all the times Mr. Jervis swerved his Scout and gunned the engine, acting like he was going to run us down? Maybe he was serious. Maybe *we* could be dead, too." Bobby Foley rolls his eyes at her, but she doesn't seem to catch it.

Pinky steps out of the classroom, seemingly oblivious to her surroundings. She lifts her hand to her chin and pats her birthmark, and I wonder if she's remembering the stolen kiss in the community center, when I'd stroked it. She bends in half and proceeds to throw up in the hallway, spewing oatmeal and banana.

Poor Pinky; she's too much of an outcast. While having kissed the dead kid might have given her some street credibility for a while, barfing in the hallway is going to negate any boost her popularity might have gotten from my death. I'm touched, though, that she's so upset—I can't say I was very nice to her, but apparently I didn't leave her with any hard feelings. Oatmeal and banana, though. Yick. *That* was a poor breakfast choice this morning.

Bobby Foley is another story. He is clearly furious—no, *outraged*—at everything that is happening to him, and Mr. Wild catches the brunt of it.

"I can't believe you would call me into a classroom with these losers—as if I was even in the same *league* as them! And why should I care if stupid old Cursive Lice is dead? Will I shed a tear over Curtis? Hell, no." Bobby is punctuating every other word by punching a fist into his palm. "I can't believe that pussy went and died so fucking *spectacularly*! Now everybody's going to be talking about him. You know, I'm pretty sure that asshole killed my dog. Fucking psycho."

Mr. Wild lays a calming hand on Bobby's shoulder. "Now, Bobby, I'm sure he didn't kill your dog. Curtis was one of the meekest kids I ever saw. Why on earth would you even think that?"

"I don't remember *why*, but I'm pretty sure I knew it was him. It was a long time ago," he adds, as if to explain his memory loss. Personally, I'm pretty sure it was George, our friendly neighborhood mass murderer, who ran over Lady all those years ago, but I'm in no position to inform Bobby of this. Bobby is not going to let Mr. Wild defuse his anger. No, Bobby storms, I was a dumbass loser and a lowly piece of shit and I have no right—none—to garner all of this attention!

And then for Stinky Pinky to go and blow chunks right outside the door of the classroom they're in?

"You're in for some primo payback," Bobby roars at Pinky. He steps over the pool of vomit, then turns and kicks the puddle back on her. Chunks of regurgitated oatmeal splatter across her face and chest. She stares at him, hands out, pleading; fat tears roll silently down her face.

"I don't care," he mutters. He obviously doesn't give a fuck about retarded Stinky Pinky or her dead fucking friend. Bobby Foley stalks off, ignoring Mr. Wild's calls for him to stop. "Fuck them all," he blows, and punches a locker as he rounds the corner.

I didn't exactly expect Bobby to be broken up at the news of my death, but really, this was a little much. I start to follow him down the hall, just to see if he's maybe going to get in a fight. Or should I stay back here, see if Pinky's okay? … Hello, what's this? One of the world's greatest mysteries is before me: the girls' bathroom. And I am finally in the perfect position to explore its great secrets without consequence.

To hell with Bobby and Pinky. They can wait.

I poke my head in gingerly. I don't really know what to expect, but I don't want to get a full view of someone taking a dump, that's for sure. Wait a minute. They get *six* stalls? How is that fair?

At one of the mirrors above the sinks, Marcy Middleton is putting on lip gloss. She leans in to apply it carefully, then pulls back, puckering. She's just smacking her lips together to coat them evenly when Nicole Hoyt and Jessica Beaulieu come in.

"I heard that Curtis was hiding in a closet when it happened," Nicole says. Marcy glances up and makes eye contact in the mirror with Nicole.

"What's that?" Marcy asks, eyebrows raised.

"You didn't hear? Sally and Curtis Price were murdered by their stepdad over the weekend! The guy came back to Osprey Falls and hid out in their old house for a couple of days until the police found him. I bet he came back to kill a few more people," Nicole says, nodding knowingly at Jessica and Marcy. "Why else would he hide out in The Meadows?" Her nose wrinkles up at this last statement. Marcy swallows hard.

"You okay?" Jessica asks, apparently noticing that Marcy looks a little pale. "Were you *friends* with them?" Her tone is incredulous; I'm sure she can't imagine super-popular Marcy Middleton hanging out with anyone so low on the social scale as us Prices.

"I had freshman English with Curtis," Marcy says quickly. "I didn't really know him, but we always said 'hi' in the hallways." She stuffs her lip gloss into her purse without realizing she's left the top off. She'll eventually have to throw out that purse, unable to get the oily stain in "kissable peach" out of the cloth.

Marcy says goodbye to Nicole and Jessica and walks briskly out of the bathroom, through the hallway, and down the outside front steps of the school. Do I have anything better to do? Nah. I tag along. She breaks into a jog and heads into downtown Osprey Falls. Eventually, she winds up at the library and collapses on the bench where I once sat to pore over the pages of *Flesh*. The irony is not lost on me, but Marcy, of course, can't possibly know how many hours I wasted away in the very spot where she is now. She buries her head into her hands and cries.

It is Bobby Foley, spiteful, furious Bobby Foley, who finds her there. He, too, has left school, apparently too pissed off at my attention-getting death to even try to sit through classes. I watch him take in the sight of this beautiful girl, her red curls shaking as she weeps, and his shoulders soften; the hard lines of his frown letting loose ever so slightly. He slides onto the bench next to her and slowly, carefully, draws her to him. She looks up at him, her eyes watery yet still a stunning green, like the grass at dawn.

"I didn't know you were so close," Bobby says. His brow creases a moment, presumably at the thought of Marcy and me hanging out together. I want to tell him that we *weren't* close; didn't he remember that he'd beaten the snot out of me to ensure that exactly that situation *didn't* happen?

Marcy articulates what I cannot. "We weren't. I'm pretty sure he liked me, though. He'd get this stupid, moony look on his face whenever I'd catch him staring at me in class. The point is, I could've made the effort to get to know him. But I didn't bother." She sighs as a maudlin shudder runs through her shoulders.

"I grew up with him, you know," Bobby starts, then pauses. He's probably trying to figure out how much he should reveal. I know what I'd do: just tell the parts that will elicit the most sympathy. Not for nothing, but Marcy's a fox, and pretty vulnerable right now. Bobby continues. "We were best friends when we were kids."

That's credible, right? For a brief time, weren't we? I'm surprised to realize he's telling the truth.

"Oh, Bobby, I didn't know," Marcy whispers, staring at him. "I never saw you two hanging out. What happened?"

"You know, the usual. We got a little older and our interests changed. I was more in to sports, and he liked ..." he stops for a moment. Does Bobby even know what my interests had been? "Comic books," he finishes.

Son of a gun. He did know, that big old softy ... then I remember. There was a day in the cafeteria when he'd come over to Al's and my table, ripped the Wolverine drawing out of my hands, and shredded it in front of me, letting the bits of paper shower down on me. I guess he'd actually glanced at the sketch before he'd shredded it.

Marcy strokes his cheek. I can almost hear him thinking that *yes, I deserve this*; he had known me, maybe had hated me, but had lost me just the same. Even Batman would mourn the Joker, right? He deserves a little sympathy. A little sugar. He and Marcy begin kissing, softly, and I can only hope that Bobby Foley is now finding himself in the uncomfortable position of being grateful to me. After all, it is my death that's helping him finally score with the cosmically beautiful Marcy Middleton.

I'm happy for the two of them. I bear no ill will toward Bobby Foley now that I'm dead. In the grand scheme of things, it was his father who made him who he is, and he can't help but be an asshole. Plus, Bobby was not the biggest asshole in my life: that honor clearly goes to George. The fact that Bobby Foley actually remembered that we'd been best friends as kids gives me hope. Maybe he'll be able to overcome his assholeness someday. On top of that, the news that Marcy was well aware that I'd had a crush on her is not as mortifying as I would've expected it to be. It's okay that she never made an effort to befriend me.

I had Penny, after all.

37.

Penny leaves her bed only once on the day after finding out about my death, and that's to pee. Otherwise, she's lying down, comforter wrapped around her so that only her eyes and the tip of her nose peek out. Her father checks on her several times, and when he's not in her room, he's on the phone. Al comes in and sits with Penny periodically, but he isn't saying much in the way of comfort, either: I'm sure he's dealing with his own dark clouds.

Around two, Mr. Paradise returns to Penny's room. "Come on, you two," he says to Penny and Al, who both take a moment to slowly focus on him. "We're going out."

Penny shakes her head. "Not going," she mumbles. Her father smiles gently at her and peels back her comforter. "No choice," he says, and the no-nonsense tone of his voice leaves no room for argument. Mr. Paradise pulls out a pair of jeans from the heap of clothes on his daughter's floor and sorts through the mess until he finds one of his old sweatshirts. "I've been looking for this," he mutters but tosses it on the bed for Penny to put on. "Come on, Al. Do you want to stop by your house for some clothes, or are you good like that?"

Al's still wearing the tan Dockers and button-down shirt he had on when Penny and Mr. Paradise called him with the news the day before. He lifts up an arm and sniffs. "I'm okay, if you've got a T-shirt I can borrow," he says. Mr. Paradise nods and leaves the room to find something that will fit Al. Penny shuffles off to the bathroom with the clothes her father has picked out for her bunched in her arms. When she comes out ten minutes later, she's dressed and her hair is combed, but her red eyes betray the fact that she's been crying again.

They pile into Mr. Paradise's car. He drives them to the youth center in town, where earlier I'd heard him call ahead to make an appointment with a counselor for the both of them. Penny starts to object when they pull into the parking lot, but her father holds up one of his paw-like hands and silences her. "You're going in," he says with finality, and she and Al both meekly comply.

I follow Penny, but when she gets into the room with the counselor, her wailing shakes me to the core. "Tell her it's okay!" I plead with the counselor, but he says little, just hands her Kleenex. I throw myself on the couch with the distraught Penny. "I'm all right. You're all right. I love you," I shout in frustration. Nothing helps. She is inconsolable. "I love you," I repeat again, then sulk next to her, both of us trapped in our misery.

An hour and a half later, the Paradises and Al are on their way home. Mr. Paradise stops at the Country Market, runs in, and returns in about fifteen minutes with a couple of bags. "Ice cream," he explains when Penny looks at him curiously. "I don't feel like cooking tonight, and I'm willing to bet you don't feel like eating. But maybe a pint of chocolate chip cookie dough will change your mind."

"Works for me," Al says.

38.

At the kitchen table, Mr. Paradise pokes at his ice cream, Al eats his methodically, scoop by scoop, and Penny stirs hers, making a soupy cookie dough mush.

"How did your counseling session go?" Mr. Paradise asks.

"M'kay," Al says, but he's not the one Mr. Paradise is really asking.

Penny glares at her father. "It sucked, okay? It fucking sucked! I cried most of the time while the guy told me my reactions were perfectly normal, that I'm still in shock, and that even though I don't believe it now, things *will* get better. I wanted to die. I still want to die. I keep thinking I can call Curtis to talk to him about all this, and then I remember he's dead, and it hurts all over again. This whole thing sucks!"

"Well," Mr. Paradise says. Then again, "Well." He takes a breath. "Penny, I'm not going to tell you things'll get better, or that I understand what you're going through, because I don't. But I do love you, and you're my daughter, so I need to make sure I do everything possible to help you get through this. So I hate to break it to you, but you're going back to the counselor tomorrow. And the next day. Every day for a year, if that's what it takes."

Penny pushes up from the table, her chair making a sickly scraping sound as it slides against the linoleum floor. "Fuck you, Dad," she says, and storms off to her room, slamming the door.

"I talked to Curtis's father today," Mr. Paradise calls out.

There's about a minute of silence, then Penny quietly slinks back into the kitchen. She leans against the refrigerator, arms crossed.

"Sit down if you want to hear this," he says, gesturing to her chair. Penny sits, scowling.

Well played, Mr. P, I think. *Let her blow up at you and reel her back in with information.* I'm a little surprised he's talked to Dad, though. How had I missed that phone call? Probably mooning over Penny curled up in her comforter, I decide.

Mr. Paradise relates his phone conversation. "The police won't release the bod—Curtis and Sally and Mrs. Price," he quickly amends, "until they've finished their investigation. Mr. Barracato—that's Curtis's father—thinks it'll be three or four days. So he's planning on Friday, maybe Saturday for the funerals. He thought it would be appropriate to bury them here in Osprey Falls, so I mentioned that cemetery you two liked to go to, Penny. That one over on Linwood? He's going to see if he can get a plot for them there. He's in Connecticut now, but his ex-wife Heidi is on her way to Osprey Falls. I guess she's helping him with all this. They'll be in touch once something's definite."

Penny's eyes are thick with tears again. If it had been any other day, any moment prior to the very one when she found out I was dead, I'm sure she would've been terrified that her father knew about our visits to the cemetery. Her eyes well.

"Thanks, Dad," she wails, and gets up to hug him tight. They hold on for a long time. Her tears soak his shirt collar, but he doesn't let her go. The scene makes me smile. I hope, for just a moment, that this is an indication that they might get through this after all.

Around dusk, Al mentions that he should probably head home to check in with his parents. Mr. Paradise agrees. I wonder if either of them have noticed that Al's parents haven't called once since Al's been at Penny's house. "You're welcome to stay here tonight, if you need to," Mr. Paradise offers, but Al shakes his head.

"Thanks, Mr. P. But I should probably call Julie, and I know my ma's going to want me to go to school tomorrow. I'll be okay," he adds when Mr. Paradise puts a hand on his shoulder. "I'm tougher than I look."

Yeah, right, you big baby, I think, but I think it with love.

39.

Al and I are surprised to find his mother uncharacteristically kind when he gets home, though I notice this benevolence starts only after Al assures her that he plans to go to school the next day. She even offers to go to the funeral with him, once the day is set, of course, and provided she doesn't have to work. He thanks her, kisses her cheek—also uncharacteristic—and heads up to his room. He talks to Julie for an hour, assures her he's doing okay, and changes into a T-shirt and boxers before climbing under the covers. He turns out his light and listens to his Walkman in the dark, playing a Guns-n-Roses cassette. He starts to sniff quietly, but soon he's blubbering. "I'm sorry, Curtis. I'm so sorry," he whispers, and my heart breaks for him. Sure, we hadn't talked as much since I'd moved, but for chrissake, we'd been best friends since the sixth grade. A couple of unreturned phone calls or ignored letters couldn't take that history away from us. His room is full of Dungeons & Dragons battle grids and maps, his new passion that he plays with Danny Evans all the time. But there are notebook pages taped up to the wall of Gambit and Wolverine, Psylocke and Rogue. *We* made those, sketched out the fantasy worlds of a million other teenage boys just like us. Can't take that away from us, brother.

Shit. I wish I'd written a will and left him the Venom statue. Al would've appreciated that.

The next day, Al and I head to school, and we get a taste of what his new "normal" is going to be. Guys like Tom Jacobs and Phil Hamlin actually say hello to him in the hall. These are cool guys; Tom plays football with Bobby Foley, and Phil is actually in a *band*. The band isn't very good, but who cares? These are classmates that have ignored Al his entire life, who seem to have just now realized that he exists among them. He almost seems—dare I say it?—popular. *You're welcome, man*, I think. This … is … awesome!

The girls are even better. Sure, some of them like Amy Bryce and Hillary Lombardo burst into tears when they see him, which is unsettling. But a lot of them—hell, I count no less than ten of them throughout the day—smile shyly, maybe a little nervously, at him in study hall and sociology class. *You're a celebrity, my friend,* I think. Best friends with the murdered kid. *Enjoy it while it lasts, and I hope for your sake, it lasts a while.* I don't think Al has ever had so many people be nice to him in his whole life.

Danny Evans catches up to him after third period and claps him on the back. "There's my man," he says. Danny is tall, with hair so light it looks almost white, and his whole body is covered in pale freckles. He's as much of a geek as Al is, but it seems that he, too, is climbing the social ladder, just by being amigos with the dead guy's friend. Al doesn't seem to notice that Danny hasn't asked him how he's doing, but I do.

"Jody Lamb just asked me if I wanted to meet her at the library after school. Can you believe it?"

Al shakes his head, offers him a weak grin. Then Danny makes a mistake.

"I'm tellin' ya, your friend Curtis getting his brains blown out is the best thing that's ever happened to me," he says. I see Al's whole body stiffen, and his cheeks flush red with anger.

"What?" Al sputters, like he's not sure he actually heard what he did, in fact, just hear.

"Hey, man, you know what I mean," Danny says, shrugging. "Not that I wished the guy dead or anything. But hell, *everyone* wants to talk to me now. 'How's Al doing?' 'Did you hang out with him, too?' 'What was his stepfather like?' And by everyone, I mean the ladies." Danny smirks.

For the first time in his life, his whole, asthmatic, dumped-on life, Al's fleshy hand clenches in to a hard fist. He throws his very first punch. It breaks Danny's nose.

I can't believe it. I've never been more proud of Al than I am right in this moment.

Danny goes down, crying, but Al just stands over him, shaking. A crowd starts to form around them, though Al doesn't seem to hear or see them. Eventually Mr. Wild elbows his way in to break it up. He makes Nicole Hoyt escort Danny to the nurse while he himself takes Al by the arm to head to the principal's office.

Principal Gillman chalks the whole incident up to Al's fragile state of mind. He announces he's sending him home without so much as a warning. The principal's office can't reach Al's parents, so Al meekly asks if maybe they could contact Mr. Paradise to come get him. They do, and he does, bringing Penny with him. She's curled in the back seat; I'm guessing Mr. Paradise doesn't want to leave her home alone. When Al timidly tells them both what happened, Mr. Paradise lets out a low chuckle. Al raises his eyebrows at him.

"Think about it, Al," he says slowly. "Danny was all excited about the attention he was getting, courtesy of you and Curtis. I'm pretty sure once word gets out that you broke his nose and he bawled in front of all those witnesses, well . . . his Casanova days have probably ended before they even started. High school kids can be rotten," he reasons, "but sometimes, karma happens."

From the back seat, Penny giggles. Not long. Not loudly. But one short, sweet giggle.

It's enough.

40.

Mr. Paradise stops at Al's house so he can grab an overnight bag of clothes. That afternoon, Dad arrives in town, and he and Heidi agree to meet up with the Paradises and Al. Dad looks awful: pale, shaky, like an old man. Heidi is tall and glamorous in comparison, with her sleek, blonde ponytail, smart skirt and suit jacket. They don't hold hands; Heidi is clearly not going to let Dad use this tragedy as a reason to get back together.

Heidi greets Mr. Paradise and introduces herself. "I'm so sorry," she says. "I didn't know them. Stephen and I were married for five years, but he never wanted to introduce me to his kids." Dad shoots her a withering stare. "It was hard, trying to find the time," she amends. "But I'm here now to try and make up for past mistakes. I was shocked when Stephen called to tell me," she says, looking at Dad again, dark pity in her eyes. "We hadn't spoken in so long. I figured the least I could do was put aside my petty pride and grudges—" she looks apologetically at Mr. Paradise. "Sorry, that's not your concern now. I just always wanted to meet Curtis and Sally. I tried to send cards, you know, for birthdays and holidays …" her voice trails off. "I just want to do the right thing by them. That's all," she finishes.

Dad's looking down, his brow furrowed. He looks so old. When was the last time I actually saw him? Christmas, seven, eight years ago? Maybe.

Mr. Paradise welcomes them into his house and offers them coffee. He introduces them to Penny and Al, and Heidi hugs them both. "I'm so glad your father reached out to us," she tells Penny. "It's nice to meet Curtis's friends, the people who were closest to him. We're going to meet Hardy Keller later, learn a little more about what Sally was like. We—we didn't know them that—" Heidi breaks down.

I wish I could tell her that it's all okay, and that she can lay off of Dad, too. I'm sure I would have liked her if we'd met, plus, the checks she sent on special occasions were often the highlight of the month for us, discussed in amazed whispers for several weeks. "Heidi sent me a hundred bucks for my birthday," Sally would gush, planning how she'd spend it before it was even cashed. And I'd get mad that I'd have to wait five whole months before *my* birthday to get the same prize. No, Heidi should ease up. We didn't expect much from either her or Dad. The fact that she consistently did more than was expected—thought of us on special days, sent a card and a note and that all-important money—was enough. She was special to us in her own way.

"He looks just like me," Dad says, looking at a framed picture from prom that Penny has laid out on the table. He stares at my picture, all tuxedo tails and smiles. "I remember . . . I found a Wonder Woman Barbie doll at a flea market once," he says. "I gave it to Sally that Christmas. She couldn't have been more than eight." He looks up, but not at anyone; rather, he's staring out the kitchen window, but his eyes aren't focused. "Curtis—I don't know—maybe I gave him a football that year. Something appropriate for a little boy, I'm sure. Well, when Sally opened that doll, she was so excited. Took it right out of the packaging and started playing with it. Problem was, Curtis wanted one, too. He positively *screamed* when she wouldn't let him play with it. A Barbie doll. I thought for sure he'd turn out gay," he said.

Jeez, Dad, thanks for *that* story. You got my sister what was essentially a superhero action figure, and I wanted one too? Go figure. And now I'm kind of regretting calling him after my first wet dream. I'm sure that just sealed the deal in his mind.

"Um, no, he wasn't gay," Penny says in a muted voice. "Definitely not," she adds, and her father looks at her, eyebrows raised. She shrugs at him.

"I'm seventeen, and *I* want a Wonder Woman Barbie," Al adds. "That kinda sounds cool as hell. And no, also not gay," he says, thrusting his chin up. Dad looks at Al, then back at Penny.

"I just … didn't know. I didn't know my kids at all," he says, and puts his hands over his face. His shoulders shudder.

This is my father. One half of my genetic makeup, the man who Mom would often dejectedly remark that I looked just like, then amend it with "but sweeter." Where had he been? Why hadn't he bothered with us? Why is he bothering now? Surely Penny and Al knew me better, certainly knew my habits and hobbies, would know what would be most appropriate for my funeral, at least. Then it dawns on me. That *is* why Dad's here. He didn't know his children, and now that the responsibility of burying us has been dumped in his lap, he's trying to find out more about who we were, and how to honor our memory.

This might be the first decent thing he's done for us in a decade.

Over coffee and potato chips, Dad, Heidi, Penny, Al, and Mr. Paradise plan our funerals. They'll hold it at the congregational church down the road from the library. They decide to have one funeral for the three of us. Penny is biting her nails absently, and I wonder if she's thinking that if Sally and I were to each have our own separate service, nobody would come. Except for Dottie down at Sunny Brook, the entire composition of my social group is sitting right here at the kitchen table. Sally hung out with even fewer people than *I* had: In the months after the abortion, before the move, she hadn't worked, hadn't gone out with friends, rarely left the house at all. I wish I'd seen that then. Made her tag along with us sometimes, just to get her back out in the world. I picture her beaming and flirting with Doogie the day after we moved to Connecticut. At least she was happy at the end of her life, I think. At least she got that.

Dad has secured a small family plot at Linwood Cemetery, just like Mr. Paradise had suggested. Heidi is footing the bill for everything: the funeral home, the priest who will hold the services, the burial plots, the catered reception afterwards. Jeez, I *really* like her. I can't believe Dad let her get away.

Heidi asks Penny if she and her father would consider sitting with the family. Penny's ever-present tears start to fall again. Dad looks over at Mr. Paradise, who nods. They agree that the family pew will be Dad, Heidi, Mr. Paradise, Penny, Al, his mother, and Julie. Dad says that Mom has a few cousins somewhere, Julia and Harry, or Larry, he thinks, but he doesn't know how to reach them. Heidi asks if perhaps they should invite Hardy Keller to sit with them too. Penny shakes her head; I never told her the details of what happened with Sally and Hardy, about the aborted baby, but she does know that it was their breakup that made Sally retreat into her room for months before the move. Whatever happened, she does know that Hardy didn't treat Sally very nicely, and she says as much.

Penny digs out some more photos so all of them can go through them and see if there's anything they can use for the funeral. Nobody thinks open caskets are a good idea. Penny worries that the pictures won't be of much help, but then she finds the one of me, Sally, and Mom on her and George's wedding day. I'm in a suit, squinting at the sun; Mom and Sally are smiling, heads tilted towards each other, looking beautiful and young and unaware of the horror that they'll face at the hands of the man Mom just married. It's perfect. Penny fishes out the negative and hands it over to Heidi gingerly.

"Please be careful with this," she whispers, hesitant to hand over any last scrap of our time together, like the photo evidence that I'd once been alive and happy might disappear, taking her memories with it. Heidi takes it gently and promises nothing will happen to it.

They decide to order food for sixty people for the reception in the church cafeteria basement afterward. Al and Penny think sixty is a high estimate, but Mr. Paradise agrees with Heidi that sixty sounds fine. Why break it to Dad and Heidi now that the Prices, really, hadn't had many friends in town? We'd been isolated by our own poverty, routines, and one impulsive kiss with Stinky Pinky in front of a window in the community center. Mom had her job and George, though "some of the Emerald crowd might come by to pay their respects" Penny muses out loud. This is what she has been reduced to: hoping the local drunks stop by to eat up the catered food at her dead boyfriend's funeral. The thought appears to be too much for her, and she apologizes to Dad and Heidi, then retreats back to bed.

41.

Our mass funeral is set for Saturday. Al has stayed with the Paradises for most of the week, and he misses his all-important geometry exam Thursday, but Friday night, he and Julie go out to see a movie. They decide on *Goodfellas*, but the unapologetic violence, the alarming number of people who are shot to death with no apparent thought, is just too much for him to take. He tells Julie he'll be in the lobby, then goes into the men's room to throw up.

Julie's in the lobby waiting for him when he comes out. She's full of apologies and tears, but Al waves her off. She couldn't have known that the movie would be that brutal. Watching them, I feel bad for Al. In the past week, it's become evident that Julie doesn't really understand what he's going through, keeps saying and doing the wrong thing without intending to. It's not a good sign. I suspect they're going to break up soon. Al gives her a quick peck on the lips when he drops her off. I hope he can hold off breaking up with her until after the funeral, at least. I think it'll be better for him if she's there with him.

On Saturday morning, Al comes downstairs wearing the suit his mother bought him for his aunt's wedding this past spring. His mother is in the kitchen, wearing a white polo shirt and a tennis skirt.

"Um, Ma, you do remember that the funeral is this morning?" he asks in a puzzled voice.

"Oh, Albert, I'm sorry. I just don't think I can bear to go. It's too much for me. You understand, don't you, peach?" She kisses the air on either side of his cheeks and flounces out of the kitchen.

Al turns red. He strips off his suit jacket as he heads to his car to go pick up Julie. I slide in the seat next to him. *Too much for her to bear? Wow, what a bitch,* I think. Last fall, Al and I had talked about what would come next, after high school. I was planning on EMT school, but Al had the money and the grades for college. He'd thought he would stay close to home, to Julie, maybe go to UMaine at Augusta or maybe Husson. *Fuck that shit,* I think, trying to will the thought into his head. *UCLA is full of hot chicks, beautiful beaches, and best of all, no parents. Hot chicks and no parents, Al! Get the hell out of Dodge!* Al stomps on the gas, leaving rubber in his parents' driveway as he squeals his tires. Okay, maybe he didn't receive my telepathic message, but the passion with which he just booked out of his parents' driveway gives me hope.

Al and Julie arrive at the congregational church fifteen minutes before the funeral is set to begin. I'm surprised to see the lot is almost full; Al takes a spot that is labeled as reserved for the pastor. He and Julie spot Penny and Mr. Paradise behind the church and hurry over to them.

"Parking's a little hairy, huh?" he says. "How're you holding up?" He gives Penny a hug.

"I'm here," Penny shrugs, putting out her cigarette on the church's sidewalk. She dyed her hair black last night to match the long black dress she's wearing. She's clutching a black lace shawl like a shroud. Her father made her take a Xanax this morning. It's not helping: She's still trapped in a nightmare. My stomach flip-flops. My girl looks smokin' hot … and she's miserable. Because of me.

Well, this sucks.

"Let's get inside to the entryway," Mr. Paradise says. "Nobody in Osprey Falls knows Mr. Barracato—I'm sure he'll appreciate the help and the familiar faces." He escorts his daughter inside, Julie and Al trailing behind.

They find Dad and Heidi right inside the oaken double doors of the church. Dad's face is a storm cloud, thundery and gray. Heidi stands next to him, hand lightly resting on his shoulder. Behind them, at the end of the center pew aisle, up by the pulpit, are three coffins. Penny glances toward the caskets, then looks away quickly.

The curiosity is too much for me to stand. I've got to look inside the closed casket.

By chance, my coffin is the first one I come to. I peek in through the top and see I'm wearing an unfamiliar suit jacket—must be one of Dad's—and the Twisted Sister T-shirt Penny gave me right before I started school in Chesterbury. The mortician did a nice job on the bullet hole, because all I can see is a slight dent in the center of my forehead. Impressive.

I spot my old stuffed dog, Clem, tucked in above my left shoulder. Sweet! I loved that dog. Nice touch; I wonder who thought of it? Dad, maybe? I then notice the Venom statue, which has been placed carefully between my hands. I guess someone figured since I'd been clutching it at the moment of my death, I must've been *really* attached to it. I look at the anguished monster rising from the black goo, a look of menace and grisliness on its face. It's repulsive. That's really not appropriate at all. Who can I talk to about this?

My own coffin was disturbing enough; I don't think I can stomach peeking in on Mom and Sally. Lord only knows what's been tucked in with them. A vodka bottle for Mom? George's old air rifle for Sally? Better to stick by Penny's side today; no more side trips.

A couple of people have started to filter in. Dottie comes up the steps, blowing her nose and blustering. She engulfs Penny in her arms, swathing her with her big frame.

"Oh, Penny. I can't believe he's gone. How're you managing? You look beautiful, which I'm sure you don't want to hear right now, but honestly, you're stunning. Mrs. Fay and Mr. Peterson wanted to come, but arranging transportation from Sunny Brook and just the whole situation … I think it would've been too much. But they send you their love. I'm so sorry. I'm sorry," she repeats again and starts blubbering. Al takes her by the arm and guides her to a pew. Penny blinks and looks at her father.

"I *can't* do this," she says, and her father smiles.

"You're handling yourself fine so far. Do it for Curtis," he adds.

More people begin to come in. Some of my old teachers, like Mr. Wild and Mr. Durden. My old art teacher, Miss Soling. Mrs. Downs, my fifth grade teacher, comes in looking gray and regal. She pats

Penny's arm and makes her way in. There's Mrs. Meisner, the Osprey Falls librarian, the one that always called me Carl. Bobby Foley escorts Marcy Middleton into the church. He's quiet and handling Marcy like she's a delicate rose, afraid she'll lose a petal if he jostles her ever-so-slightly. I'm impressed that he showed up. More signs that he's not a total asshat after all.

Still the people keep coming. Some of Sally's old crowd comes: Jack Robertson, Elaine Jessop, Tom Webber, Rusty Graves, Carla Devas. Old boyfriends: Derek Lombardo, Steve Jones; even Hardy arrives, looking somber and sheepish. As the pews fill up, Penny looks at her father, a question in her eyes: *Where are all of these people coming from?*

Still there are more. Two motorcycles loudly rumble into the parking lot and manage to find parking on the grass. Had I known anybody who was secretly in a motorcycle gang? As they casually swing off of the bikes and approach the entrance in matching gaits, I recognize them: Danny and David Ewing. Dave is clearly back from overseas, but there's no sign of his German bride. Out front, they meet up with Mrs. Ewing and Peggy and exchange hugs, then enter together as a family. Pinky arrives with Wanda Wilkes. Becky Billows, our old babysitter, steps into the line of mourners, bouncing a baby of her own on her hip. Al shakes hands with his Uncle Roy, the man with the endless supply of hockey tickets and ringside seats for wrestling. Some of the kids from town: Brad Schoonover, Eric Vaslyn. Jeff Watts. Matt Phillips. All of the guys Sally once classified as un-dateable.

A thin lady with black hair pulled tightly in a bun approaches Penny. She's escorting two young women who are probably only a year or two younger than me. "I'm Renee Allen," she explains, shaking Mr. Paradise's hand, then hugging Penny. "I've seen you around Sunny Brook. Curtis took such good care of my stepfather when he was there. Louis Valley?" she prompts, and Penny nods, stupefied. "These are my girls, Amy and Jenna. Their grandfather talked about Curtis all the time. Always took the time to listen to Dad, look at his pictures. We had to come pay our respects." She herds her girls into the church, which is quickly becoming standing room only. And still they come.

A stunning ebony woman with cropped black hair walks in, holding a young girl of maybe four firmly by the hand. The little girl's hair has been wrangled into two ponytails. She has extra elastic bands all through her pigtails, so it looks like she has two chains of silky black cotton balls sticking out of her head. Penny doesn't know the woman or the child, but I do: Here is Jill Jackson, all grown up, looking as luscious as I remembered from my youth.

Two guys are jostling to get in through the church doors. A quiet girl in a short, black dress and wearing too much eyeliner waits behind them. One of the guys spots Penny and comes over, holding out his hand. "You must be Curtis's girlfriend," he says solemnly. His serious tone doesn't quite match his outfit, which consists of black jeans, a black leather jacket, and a black and white bandanna across his forehead. "I'm Corona. Eric and me—and that's Emily behind him, she insisted on tagging along—we were friends with Curtis. In Connecticut. We thought we'd make the drive up, you know, honor our brother and all that." He's playing the role of Ambassador from Connecticut to the hilt. Al's eyebrows shoot up, but he comes over and shakes Corona's hand.

"Thanks for coming," he proclaims. His eyes fill, which is not something he wants these nonchalant, confident guys to see. Corona spots it and claps Al on the back.

"Sorry for your loss, man. We'll hang out after the service, exchange stories," he assures him. Al nods gratefully.

"I guess I didn't realize he might've made friends," Al whispers to Penny. "They're so much cooler than I am."

"Stop it," Penny says. "You were his best friend. Now shut up and help me."

It's time to go in. Hymns are played, and the pastor gives a lovely speech. Penny is invited to the pulpit to read a Robert Frost poem. She breathes deeply, steeling herself, and makes her way forward. She pauses at the coffins, then lays a soft hand on my casket. The charm bracelet I'd given her for her birthday last year jangles down her wrist and clinks against the wood. She lifts her hand to kiss the palm, then touches my casket again. She steps up to the podium and looks out.

A sea of faces gazes back: some crying, some smiling in encouragement, all waiting. She begins to read, voice wavering at first, then gaining strength. Here it is: the proof that I'd existed, I'd mattered, I *was*.

At the reception afterwards, Penny makes her way through the crowd, stopping occasionally to accept murmurs of condolence. The platters of food have been demolished, yet people still continue to hang out. I stick with Penny, hearing what she hears, seeing what she sees. She stops at a table full of Meadows kids: her curiosity and defensiveness about what Bobby Foley might be saying has gotten the best of her. She's satisfied to see Pinky is included at the table, listening to the banter.

"God, remember when Curtis fell out of that tree? You never heard a guy howl so loud! I thought he'd been impaled by a branch or something," Jill Jackson says. The Ewing twins guffaw. "What?" Jill says, looking at them.

"Um, you do know why Curtis was up in that tree, don't you?" Bobby prompts. Jill turns toward him.

"Because he was a boy, and it was a tree? Why the hell does any kid climb a tree? Because it's *there*," she says.

"Er—no, not for our boy Curtis, not exactly," Bobby says, smiling. *Now I'm his 'boy'? Am I in some weird alternate universe?* Bobby interrupts my thoughts. "He was trying to look down your top," he explains.

"What? That little shit!" Jill squeals, but she blushes, too. The table erupts in laughter, and I watch them. I grew up with these kids. I hadn't thought they'd noticed.

Penny smiles wistfully and moves on. Before following Penny, I quickly take a peek down Jill's top. My spirit soars. Still impressive.

Penny stops near the beverage table, where the picture of me, Mom, and Sally sits, blown up to 8" x 10" and framed. She picks it up and runs her fingers over my face, across my two-dimensional cheek. "I guess for most people, life just goes on," she says out loud, maybe to me. "How am I supposed to do that?"

I hate seeing her like this, caught in the land of the dead, unable to see the amazing things that are to come for her. It's going to take her awhile to swim her way past these murky waters. She doesn't think she'll make it. But I know she will.

Al's been sitting with Corona and Eric, a look of amazement on his face at the information they've shared. He breaks away to join Penny. "Did you know Curtis had started smoking? And that he was listening to, like, Metallica and shit? What the hell? It's like I didn't know him at all after he moved!" Al's voice is despondent. Penny hugs him quickly.

"Honestly, Al, I've got to take responsibility for most of that. I pushed him to try and fit in with a crowd. Bought him some heavy metal tees, sort of encouraged him to dress cooler." She smiles. "The smoking thing he picked up on his own, though. Fucker. How many times did he complain about me smoking in his truck, and he turns around …" she trails off, looks at Al again. "I guess that's not important now."

Al seems relieved. "So it wasn't like he just had some other secret life that he kept hidden from me?"

"Well, I don't know. Did *you* have any inkling that his stepfather was a murdering sociopath?" Al's face crumbles, as does Penny's. "I'm sorry," she says. "That wasn't funny." They both wipe away tears. "Come on," she says to Al. "Let's go smoke a cigarette."

"Penny … do you think you can teach *me* how to be cool?" he asks, trailing after her as they head outside.

I stay behind and look around. The crowd is impressive: kids I'd gone to school with, many who never even talked to me; grown-ups who I would've sworn never even knew my name. Tables of strangers sit now, drawn together by one act, remembering.

How can this be? How could my blip of a life and horrific death matter at all? I was invisible in the hallway, insignificant when I left. Why do these people care? Did I actually *matter*?

After all, I was just an ordinary boy.

EPILOGUE

The Osprey Falls High Class of 1991 twentieth high school reunion, held at the luxurious Osprey Falls Country Club, located on the opposite side of town from The Meadows, is not well attended. Out of the 255 kids that graduated that year, only 71 show up. Penny Paradise Donaldson is one of them.

She hadn't planned on coming. She and her husband Ken and their two children, Benjamin and Lyle, were going to go to her in-laws' house in Ohio for Thanksgiving. But then her father needed emergency bypass surgery, so she sent her family on to Ohio while she made her way back to Osprey Falls. Her father, chipper for a man who'd just had four veins from his legs grafted onto his coronary artery, reminds her about the reunion. She's bored in the hospital, and curious. Plus, she's recently lost twenty pounds, and knows she looks good. She runs out to the mall in East Bailey, finds a sexy, purple, beaded cocktail dress, and shows up at 7:30.

She's floundering for a minute, feeling awkward and lonely with nobody to talk to, but then Al walks through the door. She *thinks* that's Albert; he's thinner, both in body shape and around the hairline, but his face looks the same. Maybe a few more wrinkles and acne scars. She smiles at him, and his face brightens when he sees her.

"Penny Paradise! Wow! You look amazing," he gushes, and kisses her cheek. She hugs him. "Of course, I almost didn't recognize you with that hair. It looks so—normal," he says, eyeing her natural caramel waves that just touch her shoulders.

"Al, I'm so glad you're here. I was starting to think this was a huge mistake. Let's go find a table and catch up, okay?" She grasps his hand and leads him through the crowd to a table just off the dance floor. A waiter approaches them, and they both order a drink: a domestic beer for him, a gin and tonic for her. "So, how've you been? For, like, the past twenty years?" She laughs nervously.

"Yeah, when's the last time we saw each other? The summer after graduation, I think, right?" He smiles. "Are you on Facebook? We should be Facebook friends."

She shakes her head. "I refuse to get on Facebook. I teach eighth grade science, and I don't want my students finding me on there. When my kids are a little older, maybe I'll join just to monitor them—"

"Kids!" Al interrupts. "How many?"

"Two boys, Ben and Lyle. They're nine and six. We live in Conway, New Hampshire, just over the border. I'm married. Ken and the boys are at his parents' for the holiday." Al nods. "Where are you these days?"

"Simi Valley. California. As far away from Maine as possible," he smiles. "My wife—Eva—stayed behind this trip. She can't stand my parents," he shrugs, and Penny offers a sympathetic smile. "I can't either. But I feel obligated to see them once a year. This seemed like the perfect trip to do it. Only four days, a reunion to go to … my exposure to them is limited." He takes a swig of his beer. "I'm glad you're married, Penny. I was worried about you. You know, after Curtis …" his voice trails off.

"After Curtis," she echoes. "Yeah, well, I was kind of a mess for a long time after that. Wouldn't date anyone, and I'd blow up at any guy who even *looked* at me. Slept a lot. Didn't shower much. I was in bad shape." Her face clouds at the memory. "Dad's the one who got me through it. He pushed me to rejoin the real world. Hell, I think I was in counseling for a year," she sighs and sips her drink. "But it helped. Thank God Dad made me go."

"Your dad was pretty awesome, if I remember correctly," Al says.

"Still is," she says. "He still lives in town."

"No kidding. Tell him I said 'hello.' I've never forgotten how nice he was to me after Curtis died." He pauses. "You know, I still think of things in terms of 'before Curtis died' and 'after Curtis died.' Like, 'When did I see Culture Club in concert? That's right, it was right *before* Curtis died.'" Penny nods; she knows exactly what he means, because she does the same thing. Not as much lately; maybe not in a long time. But sometimes, when her kids are looking through her old photo albums and laughing at her pink hair, she'll look at the picture and think *that was taken about a month before Curtis died*. She never says it out loud, of course.

"Want to hear something stupid?" Al asks shyly.

"Sure," Penny shrugs.

"Did I tell you where I'm working? No? I design video games for Blizzard Entertainment. You know, those role-playing games with the warlocks and trolls and killer harpies and stuff?" he asks.

Penny smiles questioningly. "Sounds like a great job. What's stupid about that?"

"Well, the one that I worked on that came out last year, *Necromancer's Wrath?*" He sees Penny's confused look and keeps going. "It was a big hit with under-21 crowd. Won some awards from *PC Magazine*," he boasts. She shrugs apologetically. "No matter. Anyway, one of the hidden characters, you know, that you can't unlock unless you complete the Elvin Quest in under four minutes? It's a white mage. I got to design him, and I named him Curtis."

Penny laughs, relieved. "I wasn't sure where you were going with that story. A mystical fairytale mage named Curtis? That's awesome!"

Al chortles with her. "Yeah, my manager loved it. Most of those characters are named things like Baeldaeg or Freyja. He thought it was a funny little meme that the kids would eat right up. And you know, I just wanted to ... have something out there for him. To let him know I never forgot him."

Penny smiles wistfully and lays her hand over Al's on the table. "I know what you mean. My oldest son Ben's middle name is Curtis." Al looks over at her, and the two share a somber moment.

"What are you two losers looking so depressed about?" a voice breaks in. Penny looks up to see Bobby Foley. She has to admit he looks good: his salt-and-pepper hair is short, and his brown suit is cut sharply, revealing that Bobby clearly still works out.

"We're talking about Curtis," she explains. "Curtis Price. Do you remember him?"

"Of course I remember him. I lived two doors down from him, didn't I? Jeez. You two gloomy-doomers need to cheer up. Life goes on, right?" Bobby puts his drink down and pulls up a chair. "By the way, Paradise, you look smokin' hot, I must say."

Penny waves off the compliment. "So, how's life been treating you, Bobby?" She doesn't really care that much, but it's polite to ask.

"Oh, just fine. I joined the Marines right out of high school, did my tour in Desert Storm, then went to UMaine on the GI Bill. That's where I met my wife, Mandy. She's in the bathroom right now. Incidentally, don't eat the mushroom appetizers—I think that's what's bothering her."

"That's nice," Al says. He raises his eyebrows at Penny, and she can see he's having a hard time wrapping his mind around the bizarreness of this scenario. They're both at a table conversing with Bobby Foley, something that never would've happened in high school. "So what do you do?"

"I'm a paramedic," Bobby says. "Mandy's a nurse. We have two girls, Ashley and Bethany."

Penny's eyes brighten. "You know, Curtis wanted to be an EMT. Isn't that funny?"

Bobby shakes his head. "I didn't know that. Shit." He takes another mouthful of his drink and swallows hard. "I had a hard time dealing with Curtis's death, believe it or not. I just kept thinking about the time I beat him up—it was pretty bad, too. I can't for the life of me remember why. Isn't that something? I pounded the shit out of that kid, and I didn't even have a good reason. I felt guilty about that for years."

Penny puts her hand up to cover her smile. She tries to stifle a giggle but fails. Bobby looks up at her. "What?" he says, his eyes narrowing.

"I remember that. You did beat him up pretty bad. But don't you remember, two, maybe three weeks later? You had water in your gas tank one morning?"

Bobby slaps his hand on the table. "That little shit! That was him? I didn't think Cursive Lice had it in him. Goddamn." Bobby is smiling. This news has somehow made him feel better.

"Well, I helped. But it was his idea," Penny confirms.

The three of them sit for a moment, looking down into their drinks and thinking about good old Curtis Price. Bobby finally lifts his scotch on the rocks, holding it in midair. Penny and Al follow suit with their own cocktails.

"To Curtis Price," Bobby starts. "My worst enemy, but I'll admit it, I think his death probably made me a better person," he says.

"To Curtis," Al chimes in. "My best friend. He got me through some of the worst years of my life. High school would've sucked without him."

"To Curtis," Penny echoes. "My first love. Maybe the love of my life." Their glasses clink softly.

And with that, their lives go on.

ABOUT THE AUTHOR

Stacey Longo is the author of *My Sister the Zombie* and *Secret Things: Twelve Tales to Terrify*. Her stories have appeared in numerous anthologies and magazines, including *Shroud*, *Shock Totem*, and the *Litchfield Literary Review*. A former humor columnist for the *Block Island Times*, she maintains a weekly humor blog at www.staceylongo.com. Longo lives in rural Connecticut.

Made in the USA
Charleston, SC
07 June 2016